Books by Bella Settarra

The Cowboys of Cavern County

Carla's Cowboys
Maggie's Man

I0570862

Maggie's Man

ISBN # 978-1-786686-070-5

©Copyright Bella Settarra 2016

Cover Art by Posh Gosh ©Copyright 2016

Interior text design by Claire Siemaszkiewicz

Totally Bound Publishing

Published in 2016 by Totally Bound Publishing, Newland House, The Point, Weaver Road, Lincoln, LN6 3QN, United Kingdom.

The Cowboys of
Cavern County

MAGGIE'S MAN

BELLA SETTARRA

Dedication

To Annie, with lots of love. XX

Chapter One

Maggie smiled at the good-looking cowboy who had planted himself opposite her at the counter. He had come in here every day for the past few weeks and wasn't showing any signs of getting tired of her cooking — or her company — yet.

"Morning, Maggie. I'll take a coffee and one of those cinnamon buns, please." His baby-blue eyes twinkled as he removed his hat and placed it on the stool beside him.

"Coming right up. This is getting to be a regular habit, isn't it?" She grinned at him. "Not that I'm complaining, of course."

"Yeah. No one cooks like you do. It's well worth the trip." He took the plate from her, sniffing the fresh cinnamon.

"Oh, right." She felt a little disappointed.

He must have noticed her expression. "You sure know the way to a man's heart," he added quickly.

Good save. She snickered. "Well, I wish that was all it took," she joked.

He raised his eyebrows, taking a swig of his coffee. "You're not gonna tell me you're single?"

She giggled. "I sure am," she told him, admiring his subtle way of asking. "I know it's hard to believe, isn't it?" She put a hand to the back of her head, posing like a model. Sticking her nose in the air, she gave him a blasé look before bursting into laughter. She knew she was a little too old and a lot too fat to pull off a super-model appearance, but she was having fun pretending. In truth, she was still in her twenties, but she felt more like a hundred and twenty.

"I can't for the life of me imagine why you're not wed."

He sounded serious, much to her amazement.

She sighed, quickly turning away from his handsome face while wiping her hands on her apron.

"Can we get some coffees over here, miss?" An older gentleman had just sat at a window seat with a lady, whom Maggie guessed would be his wife.

"Of course." Maggie suddenly felt flustered. She hadn't taken any notice of them coming in, as she'd been too busy laughing with Aiden Fielding, the gorgeous cowboy.

Her hand shook as she poured the coffee, and she tipped one of the cups over with the edge of the coffee pot, sending the hot, black liquid running all over the counter.

"Damn!" She felt herself go hot and knew she was blushing. Panic overtook her as she quickly tried to rectify the mess.

"Hey, hey. Are you okay?" Aiden was on his feet in a second, moving everything out of the way of the stream of coffee that was threatening to engulf everything in its wake. His voice was calm and gentle, and Maggie wished she could be as composed as he was.

"Yeah, I just…" She took a cloth and soaked up the spill, surprised to see Aiden dive behind the counter and grab a clean cup.

He quickly poured the drinks and placed them on a tray while she cleaned up the counter. "Did you scald yourself?"

He was right next to her, and she was surrounded by his fresh cologne. She had admired his scent from across the counter, but he was even closer to her now, and she was immersed in the heady aroma. He was a gorgeous-looking guy and seemed to really care about her. But she had to remember he was way out of her league—and age range. Although he must have been a year or two her senior, she usually went for much older men than him—not that she'd had that many.

"Er…no. No, I'm fine. Thank you," she stammered as he stared at her with his big, concerned eyes. "I'd best take these over." She took the tray, brushing past him as she squeezed from behind the counter to serve her customers.

"I can recommend the cinnamon buns," Aiden called over to the elderly couple as Maggie served their drinks.

"Now that sounds like a good idea," the man remarked, looking first to Aiden then to his companion. "What do you think, Sylvia? Cinnamon bun?"

Maggie noticed the lady's face light up, much the same as she was sure hers did when someone mentioned food.

"Ooh, yes please." The lady smiled excitedly.

"We'll take two, please." The man nodded at Maggie.

"No problem." She quickly returned to the counter and placed two of the warm buns onto a plate. She loaded up the tray with knives and side plates, as well as a couple of napkins then smiled at Aiden before taking them over to the couple.

"Thanks for that. You're good for business," she told the cowboy when she arrived back at the counter. He had already returned to his seat opposite her and was sipping his coffee.

"Gotta keep you employed," he said with a laugh.

"Ain't that the truth." She sighed, rolling her eyes.

He frowned. "Now that's the second time this morning I've said the wrong thing," he said, narrowing his eyes. "Is everything all right, Maggie?"

She balked, shocked that she had given away her feelings. "Oh, of course. No, you didn't say anything wrong." She tried to assure him but could see he wasn't convinced. "Everything's fine, really."

She busied herself tidying away some dishes so she didn't have to look at him, but she could feel his eyes boring into her.

"Do you like working here?" he asked after a few minutes.

She turned back to him, smiling. "Yes, of course."

She followed his gaze as he looked around the little café. It was a cozy place with red-checked tablecloths on wobbly-legged tables, surrounded by old, mismatched chairs. A couple of booths occupied one end while a row of tables stood in front of the large window. At the other end was the door to the small kitchen that backed from the counter where Maggie served coffee. Tall bar stools lined the counter from the patron's side so customers – like him – could easily perch up there and have a quick drink or chat to the waitress.

"Does it ever get busy in here?" he asked.

"Not really," she told him. "Which is just as well, being as the boss refuses to take on any more staff. He reckons I cost him enough, already. Ha!"

She thought back to the pittance she earned working here every day. Her only consolation was that it was easy work and she didn't have to travel far to get here. Trouble was, Bracken Ridge, where they were situated, was so far away from anything that they hardly had any customers. The Melrose Motel stood opposite them, but business wasn't exactly booming there either, so she didn't get many residents to cook for. Most people just drove right on through the tiny village to get to the more interesting towns of Almondine or Pelican's Heath, a short trip down the road.

"But surely if business picked up, he'd have to?" Aiden appeared thoughtful.

"Yeah right. Like that's gonna happen." She wiped her hands in her apron again. "Between you and me, it's more likely to close down altogether," she told him in a hushed tone.

Aiden looked surprised. "So where does that leave you?"

"Oh don't worry about me. I'm likely to be out of a *home* before I'm out of a job anyhow, so it won't make much difference either way."

His shocked face told her she had said too much, and she inwardly admonished herself for letting her tongue run away with her. There was just something about Aiden. He was so easy to talk to.

"Thank you very much, dear. That was lovely." The elderly couple left their table, calling over to her from the door.

"Glad you liked it. Come again." Maggie was grateful for the distraction and hurried on over to clear their table, noticing that they had left a large tip along with their payment.

When she returned to the counter, Aiden was taking a call on his cell. "Yeah, tell him we're interested," he said. "Definitely. We want that land at the best possible price, ya hear? Thanks for that."

"Everything all right?" she asked, sad to see him stand up.

"Just peachy. I'm hoping to accrue more land for the ranch, expand a little." Excitement shone from his eyes as he nodded, smiling. "Say... How about a drink tonight? What time do you finish?" He put his hat on.

She frowned in surprise. "Don't you think I'm a bit old?"

"Too old to go for a drink?"

She snickered, her heart racing. She really liked the guy, and she did enjoy his company. He had a point, though. They were only going for a drink. "Okay. I get off around seven." Something burned inside her, and she couldn't help smiling at the thought of spending more time with the hunky cowboy.

"I'll be here, then," he told her with a grin, throwing a handful of notes on the counter.

"I'll look forward to it." She was sad to see him go, but it was nice to think it was only for a few hours.

* * * *

Aiden climbed into his truck. He liked Maggie Welch a lot and was pleased that he'd finally plucked up the courage to ask her out. It had been several weeks since they'd met, and he'd liked her from the start. She always seemed quite happy and cheerful, so it was a shock to see her flummoxed and a little pensive today. Something must have happened.

He drove down the back road toward Pelican's Heath,

looking forward to seeing her again tonight. It was obvious he'd said the wrong thing when he mentioned her being married. He'd meant it as a compliment but could see he'd hit a raw nerve. And what about losing her home and job? That poor girl always seemed to put on a brave face, but it seemed things weren't quite as they appeared with her.

Ben, his older brother was waiting for him when he pulled up at the ranch. "No prizes for guessing where you've been."

Aiden grinned. "I've got a date with her tonight."

Ben hooted with laughter. "Well now, you actually did it? What in hell kept ya, bro?"

"Very funny. I just wanted to wait for the right moment. That's all. I don't think she's as confident as she makes out, you know?"

He followed Ben over to one of the meadows that looked out to the south of the Fielding Ranch.

"I can't wait to meet this one," Ben murmured, shaking his head.

"Maybe in time, bro." Aiden wasn't so sure his family would approve of Maggie.

Ben chuckled, looking out over the land in front of them. "Well, you'll sure be able to impress the girl if we get all this," he remarked.

Aiden sighed. He knew money and land weren't going to impress a girl like Maggie, and he was glad of it. He couldn't explain that to Ben, though.

"Well, I've told Walker we're interested," he said, "but at a reasonable price. We can't let this guy know how much we want it."

Ben nodded. "Yup. I don't even know this guy, Rossington. Seems he just recently acquired the spread, and now he wants to sell it on. I knew old Jake Parry had passed away, but I thought his family was keeping the place on."

"Maybe they're finding it hard to cope," Aiden mused. "Perhaps we should've offered them more help?"

"If they were anything like the old man, they'd have

had to beg for it." Ben snorted. "That old cuss wouldn't give you the time of day. He sure wouldn't thank you for offering any kind of help. Probably misinterpret it as an insult, if you ask me. No, I reckon we were right to leave well enough alone there, bro."

Aiden sighed. Ben was probably right. Jake Parry was known for not being the friendliest of men, and his family seemed to be behind him all the way. He'd been a wealthy guy, though, and owned a lot of land hereabouts. If they could just get their hands on the few acres that bordered their land, it sure would provide a much-needed boost to the Fielding Ranch.

"I'd love to see a few thoroughbreds over there," Ben remarked wistfully, pointing to one of the fields.

Aiden shook his head. "Nah, I reckon we should get more quarter horses. They're good all-rounders. And if we're gonna start giving riding lessons, as Josie suggested, they'd be perfect for the job."

Ben frowned, looking back at him. "But think what it would mean to get some more real good thoroughbreds. It'd give a good impression to folks who came to take your lessons, too. Let them see how affluent we are. We've got to make it look good, and the few we've got don't exactly stand out."

Aiden sighed. This argument was getting old. Ben had always been more interested in how things looked to the outside world, instead of what was practical.

"But we won't *be* that affluent if we go throwing good money away on show horses," he objected. "We can get more quarters for the same money, and they'll be a lot more useful to the ranch as a whole."

"Nah, we've got enough. We don't need to bring in any more, at least not yet a while. I reckon we need to lift the prestige of the Fielding a little, and the best way to do that is to buy the best."

Aiden rolled his eyes. "Well, let's think about that once we've got the land, shall we? One step at a time."

Ben nodded and smirked, which let Aiden know that, as far as he was concerned, he'd won the argument. *Damn!*

Chapter Two

Maggie was a little nervous but quite excited to see Aiden Fielding come into the café at seven o'clock sharp. He looked really cool in his tight-fighting Levi's and partially unbuttoned shirt. She was glad she'd put on a pretty floral top with her jeans today and had already combed her long blonde waves out of their tight bun, so they hung loosely around her shoulders. She'd also touched up her lip gloss and mascara, hoping it would be enough to make a good impression.

"Ready?"

She smiled. She was more than ready. She'd practically booted out the last of her customers fifteen minutes ago so she could clean up the place and primp herself a little before he arrived.

"All set." She grabbed her purse and coat from the counter then followed him out of the door, locking up on her way out.

"You look lovely." His face shone in the dim light as he beamed at her, and she felt a warmth in her stomach she hadn't felt in a long time.

"So do you." She blushed, not sure if that was the correct thing to say to a man, although it was the truth. She was a bit out of practice with this sort of thing.

He chuckled and led her over to his truck, which had clearly been washed for the occasion.

"Have you eaten?" He was holding open the door and offered her a hand to climb up into the seat.

"No, but—"

"Good. I thought we might grab a bar meal while we're

out. I'm starving." Aiden pulled her seatbelt out, and she grabbed it quickly before he could reach over and slot it into place.

"Thanks," she said, fastening it herself. She was a rather large girl and very conscious of her weight. The last thing she wanted was for him to have to heave the belt over her fat tummy. "A meal sounds great."

She watched him close the door and walk around the front of the truck. "Did you have a good afternoon?" he asked as the engine purred into life.

She nodded. The vehicle screamed quality. The leather upholstery was immaculate and the whole vehicle still smelled new. The walnut dashboard was highly polished and the seat felt soft and comfy. "How about you?"

"Great." He smiled. "Remember I said we're hoping to buy more land to expand the ranch a little? Some just came up for sale on the ranch that backs onto our south field."

"That's good." She was happy for him, although it was yet another reminder that the gorgeous guy was way out of her league.

"Yeah, only big bro has got his own ideas how to use it." He shook his head with a sigh. "He wants to get more thoroughbreds in, while I just want more quarter horses. I'm thinking of setting up a riding school over there, and the quarters will come in useful."

"Makes sense. Why does he want thoroughbreds?" she asked, intrigued.

"Same reason he wants everything," Aiden grumbled. "For show."

"Oh."

Aiden looked over at her. "He only cares about how things look from the outside," he explained. "I'd rather spend our money on stuff we need and can use. I suppose I can see that thoroughbreds are an investment, but right now we need to think about keeping up the revenue, you know? There'll be plenty of time to think about appearances once we've got the money rolling in." He sighed, tipping his hat a little farther back on his head. His fair, wavy hair fell forward onto his face.

"I'm with you on that one," she told him thoughtfully. "Go for the practicalities first. The rest can wait."

He grinned over at her. "I'm glad you can see it my way."

She watched as he drove out onto the main road and toward town. He looked real competent as he handled the large truck, and everything about him shouted class. Although he was casually dressed, he looked neat and smart. He smelled of that gorgeous cologne that she just knew was expensive. Something in his manner told her he was a guy who was used to an easy life, not having to graft for every penny. She was happy for him. She just felt sorry for herself — a trait that she hated and silently admonished herself for.

He pulled up outside a rather swanky-looking restaurant and bar.

"Am I under-dressed for this place?" She balked at the sight of it.

He grinned, leaning over the steering wheel. "Don't you know? Casual is the new smart?"

She smiled. He oozed confidence, and she couldn't help letting a little of it rub off on her. "Well, if you're sure?"

"Come on." He winked as he quickly climbed out then came around to open her door just as she unfastened her seatbelt.

She loved the feel of her hand inside his when he helped her down. "Have you been here before?" She noticed the maître d' nodding and smiling at him as he walked in.

"A few times." He grinned.

"Mr. Fielding, how nice to see you, sir. Would you like your usual table by the window?"

"That would be great, Enriqué." Aiden put his hand in the small of Maggie's back when they followed the waiter over to their table.

She waited while the maître d' pulled out her chair, then she allowed him to place her napkin on her lap.

He clicked his fingers to a waitress who brought over their menus and a wine list.

"I will leave you to study the food," he told them. "Perhaps an aperitif while you decide?"

"I'll take a sweet sherry, please, Enriqué. Whatever you've got. Maggie?" Aiden looked over at her, his eyebrows raised.

"Um, I'll have the same, thanks." She managed a smile, and the waitress and her boss disappeared.

Maggie shuffled uncomfortably. Although some of the other diners were in jeans, theirs looked a lot more expensive than hers, and the women wore designer tops with sparkling jewelry, which she guessed wasn't fake.

"Are you sure I'm not out of place?" she whispered over to Aiden.

He frowned in astonishment. "Of course not. You look beautiful, Maggie. I haven't seen you with your hair down before. It looks lovely." He smiled, and she felt a glow inside her.

She turned back to the menu in her hand. "What are you going to have?" She had already noticed the cost of the food and it left her feeling a bit sick.

"I thought I'd dive straight in with the steak," he said, a little sheepishly. "You can have a starter if you prefer, though?"

"No, no. The steak's fine. Rare, please."

He grinned, closing his menu.

The maître d' must have been watching, since he swooped down as soon as Aiden had taken her menu and put them together in one hand.

"Have you chosen, Mr. Fielding? Madam?"

"We'll both have the rump, rare with all the trimmings please, Enriqué. And a good red to go with it. Châteauneuf-du-Pape?" He looked questioningly at Maggie, who nodded. It had been a while since she had drunk anything so expensive.

As soon as Enriqué left them, Aiden stretched his hands

over the table to hers. She was surprised to feel his warmth as he tenderly stroked her fingers.

"So, tell me everything. I wanna know all about you," he said, smiling.

"There's not much to tell," she assured him, suddenly feeling a little nervous.

"Where are you from? Have you any family? What other jobs have you had? What are your plans for the future? What's your favorite color?" He chuckled, taking a sip of his sherry.

"Oh my goodness, that's a lot of stuff you wanna know," she told him with a giggle. *And nothing I want to tell you*, she thought ruefully. "Okay, my favorite color's red. What's yours?"

"Green," he said straight away.

"The color of the grass, that's nice," she mused. *The color of money*, she thought.

He nodded. "You're a real country girl, aren't you?" He smiled at her approvingly.

"Yeah." *I am now.* With her jeans and cowboy boots, he'd be forgiven for thinking that, but then, looks could be deceptive.

"And you're a country boy, aren't you?" It was a safe bet that he'd been brought up on the family ranch, although he must have considered himself the landed gentry, whereas she looked like a common hillbilly.

"Yup. Born and bred on the Fielding Ranch." He confirmed her suspicions.

"And you still live there? With your family?"

"I have a cottage on the spread. My sister, Josie, and her husband live in the main house. Ben, our older brother, prefers to live just outside of town, but he still works on the ranch." He took another sip of his drink.

"No parents?" She frowned, concerned that she might have hit a raw nerve.

"Not anymore." He smiled a little sadly, and she knew it was a sore subject.

"I'm sorry," she said. "I shouldn't have asked."

"Not at all. It's absolutely fine."

She was surprised to feel his hand tickle the back of hers and realized he must have been worried that *he'd* upset *her*. She quickly smiled at him to try to reassure him otherwise. He was really thoughtful, and she appreciated that.

"So, do you live at Bracken Ridge?"

The food arrived just then, and she was grateful for the distraction.

"Not far from the café," she told him, breathing in the aroma of the delicious meal in front of her.

The sommelier arrived with their wine, and she watched Aiden taste it. He nodded to the waiter who then poured both glasses.

"To us." Aiden lifted his glass in a toast and she reciprocated, a little surprised.

"To us," she echoed, wondering just what he meant. He was a lovely guy and she really enjoyed his company, but surely he could see there was no future for them? *More's the pity.*

The rich wine coated her throat in flavors of warm spice, herbs and a hint of game. She could tell it was a good year, maybe 2005 or 2007, she surmised, and she licked her lips as a taste sort of like hot tar danced on her tongue. She closed her eyes to savor it and was surprised to see Aiden watching her closely when she opened them again.

"You like?" he asked.

"I love," she replied, "the wine and Châteauneuf-du-Pape itself." She licked her lips to enjoy every last drop.

Aiden straightened up in surprise. "You've been there?"

She smiled, realizing he wouldn't have imagined half the things she'd done in her life, assuming as he did that she was just an old-fashioned country girl.

She nodded. "I used to love going to the south of France," she said, as a memory of long, warm hazy days spent visiting vineyards as though she were some kind of royalty crossed her mind's eye.

"The weather is beautiful, and the people are so kind and generous." She recalled how many crates of wine she and her fiancé had been given before they'd left, a sort of thank you for all the business they had sent to the little wineries.

Aiden looked impressed. "When was this? How did you come to be there? On holiday?"

"Something like that." She took a mouthful of her succulent steak and actually groaned at the taste. It had been a long time since she'd eaten anything so delicious.

"A woman of mystery," Aiden remarked.

"Not really," she said with a smile. "I've just seen a bit more of life than you and traveled farther."

His head snapped up in surprise. "You're no older than me," he protested. "Although I get that you may have done a little more with your life. I've never moved out of Cavern County."

She was pleased he was too much of a gentleman to ask a lady her age, and she just smiled. She'd guessed he lived a sheltered life of luxury.

"Does it bother you?" He looked incredulous.

"That depends," she replied, narrowing her eyes a little, "on what you've got in mind."

She felt a burn in her stomach as she watched his eyes darken. He really was a gorgeous guy, and she'd love to take things further with him, but—

"I want to see more of you."

Her pussy clenched at his deep voice, and the look in his eyes told her that he was well aware of the innuendo in his statement. She swallowed hard.

"D-do you?" She felt herself go hot and knew she was blushing. Hopefully it was too dark for him to notice, although, she remembered with a cringe, she had certainly seen him flush earlier. His expression told her that he had noticed all right.

"Is that a problem?" He stretched his hand back over the table and placed it lightly on her arm.

She bit her lip anxiously. *How do you answer that?*

19

She shook her head slowly, knowing darn well she'd love to see more of the handsome hunk – in more ways than one. "Good." He stroked her arm before removing his hand to take a sip of his wine.

She felt almost bereft at the loss of contact.

Quickly she took another sip of her own drink, gaining strength from its warm richness.

"So you know quite a bit about wine?" He continued with his meal, studying her intently.

"I know a bit," she replied nonchalantly.

"And is that something you're interested in?"

"Not especially. It's just something I've learned about over the years. When you go out there to the vineyards, they're only too keen to tell you all about it. For instance, did you know that this wine is made primarily from three types of grapes – the granache noir, the syrah and Mourvedre?"

He was about to take a sip of his drink when he put the glass back down in surprise.

"No, I didn't know that."

"The more Mourvedre they use, the more tannin you can taste in it, like in a younger wine," she went on, taking another sip.

"Well, that's fascinating," he said, his jaw looking a little slack.

She grinned, pleased that she'd impressed him.

"I'd love to travel over there," he said after a few minutes' eating.

"You should." She took another sip just before he took the bottle and refilled her glass. "I think everyone should travel."

"I might need to take a guide with me," he teased.

"I'm your man…er…woman," she pounced.

He laughed. "Yeah, I'll bear that in mind."

Her head was going a little muzzy, and she knew she'd probably drank too much wine on an empty stomach, so she tucked into her meal. The last thing she wanted was to get tipsy tonight. She'd told him way too much already…

Chapter Three

It hadn't occurred to Maggie that Aiden would want to take her all the way back to her apartment after their evening out. Of course, it should have, but she hadn't really thought that far ahead. She had only expected to pop to a local bar, have a couple of drinks and probably shell out for a cab home while he met up with some other friends, or something.

"It's just up here." She cringed. Her place was far from salubrious, and she knew he'd be shocked by it.

"Aren't there any street lights around here?" He frowned, switching his headlamps to full beam.

"No." She felt a little embarrassed. It didn't usually bother her, although there had been one or two nights lately when she'd felt that she was being followed. It was probably just her imagination, she knew, and had consoled herself that with her build she should be able to hold her own against any would-be attacker. It wasn't as if she ever carried much money — she didn't have any — so any thief would be sorely disappointed if they grabbed her purse.

"Do you drive?" Aiden asked.

"Nope." *Not anymore.*

"So you walk down here alone every night after work?"

She sighed. "Yes, I do."

He shook his head, and she watched him purse his lips as though annoyed.

"It's just this one here." She was glad to change the subject by pointing out the small apartment block on the far corner.

He looked over at the building as he pulled up outside.

"Well, thanks for a great evening." She quickly unfastened

her seatbelt, hoping to get out of the truck before him.

"I'll walk you to your door." He was frowning, and she thought it best not to argue.

She sighed, a little despondently. She really liked the guy and had had a fantastic evening with him. He was great fun as well as a perfect gentleman, but she really didn't want to ruin everything by showing him just how far apart their worlds were.

"Thank you." She took his hand as he helped her down from her seat. Then she led him toward the building while she delved into her purse for her keys.

She felt his hand in the small of her back, even through her coat, and she smiled. It was a nice, protective gesture that she really enjoyed — certainly something that she had never experienced before.

"The elevator doesn't work," she quickly informed him when he steered her toward it.

He said nothing but allowed her to lead him up the stairs. She was only a few flights up and regularly lied to herself that she was glad of the exercise.

"Do you want coffee, or...?"

Although she willed him to say no, he nodded.

Maggie took a deep breath and unlocked her front door. She just knew this would be the end of any future they might have had together, even as friends.

"Well, this is it." She flicked on the light and showed him into the tiny apartment that had been her home for the past couple of years.

He must have noticed the smell of dampness, and when he went through to the living room, the old mismatched furniture covered in musty throws to disguise the state of it must have made him want to turn around and leave right away. She watched him look around, obviously taking in the threadbare carpet, old-fashioned wallpaper peeling from the walls and the draft that whistled through the gaps in the window frames.

"Do you wanna stay for coffee?" she asked slowly, unsure

of whether he would have changed his mind, having seen how she lived.

He turned to her with wide eyes. "Yes, please."

She was surprised but relieved as she went through to the tiny kitchenette to put the pot on. The two rooms were only separated by an ancient pass-through, so she was able to watch him remove his hat and take a good look at her knickknacks.

At least he didn't turn tail and run. That's a good sign, right?

"You sure like to read," he remarked when she took the tray through.

He was standing in front of a very well-worn bookcase that dominated one wall. She wondered if he'd noted the fact that there was no television, so she didn't really have much else to do, although it suited her fine. She'd never been one to slob around in front of the TV, even when she had one in every room.

She smiled as she placed the coffees on a small table and sat down on the lumpy sofa. "Yes I do."

He perused a few titles of some very dog-eared books that she had picked up in a junk shop before his hand rested on one that looked quite pristine.

"*A Modern Guide to Social Etiquette,*" he read aloud. He pulled the book from the shelf and snickered while he leafed through the pages. "So this is how you know so much about expensive wines."

She felt herself glow hot when he teased her, and she shot to her feet.

"Not exactly," she snapped, grabbing the book from him. "You don't know anything, so don't you dare make judgments like that."

"I'm... I'm sorry, Maggie. I didn't mean—"

"Get out!" She held the book close to her chest and pointed to the door with her other hand.

"I meant it's good that you know this stuff. Self-improvement is always—"

"Out!" She'd heard enough.

He looked hurt and embarrassed as he grabbed his hat and quickly made his way toward the door.

"I'm sorry," he repeated on his way out, but she wasn't listening. She slammed the door and bolted it as soon as he'd gone, before crumbling into a heap of miserable tears on the floor beside it, still clutching her book.

* * * *

"More pancakes?"

Aiden shook his head. He really didn't feel hungry this morning. He felt sick.

"No thanks, Josie. I've had more than enough."

She rolled her eyes. "I remember a time when you used to eat twice as much as that," she remarked, gesturing to his plate.

"Think he's love-sick, sis." Ben hooted with laughter across the table.

"Very funny." Aiden was in no mood to be teased today. He yawned.

"So are we all agreed then? We'll hold a dinner party and invite this Mr. Rossington and his wife. I assume he has one?" Josie was jotting down more notes in her large diary as she spoke.

"Hmm, we'll have to invite a few others, too, so as not to look obvious," Ben offered. "I'm sure I can come up with a few influential locals that could impress him."

"It's a good idea," Greg agreed, putting a fresh pot of coffee on the table before taking a seat next to his wife. "But I don't want Josie overdoing it." He put a possessive arm around her shoulder.

"Greg, I'm pregnant, not ill," she pointed out, rolling her eyes.

"I know, but it's still early days. You have to be careful." Greg was adamant.

"Well, perhaps I could find someone to help out a little," she relented with a smile. She pursed her lips as she looked back to her diary. "How many people were you thinking of, guys?"

"Well if we're gonna schmooze the guy, we'll need to invite him and his wife, and if there's four of us, we'll need at least one other couple to balance it out, then maybe a couple more to make it look less obvious," Ben replied thoughtfully, counting them out on his fingers.

"Is that a couple or a couple of couples?" Aiden frowned, taking a sip of his coffee.

Josie giggled, her light brown curls dancing around her shoulders. She wasn't showing yet, but she sure looked radiant. "Oh I think we'll need more than a couple," she said, her eyes flashing with mirth.

"So, is that more than a couple or more than a couple of couples? Jeez, you guys." Aiden shook his head in frustration while the others laughed.

"Leave it with me. I'll drum up some guests," Ben told them with a chuckle when he got up. "Thanks for the breakfast, Josie." He leaned over the table and gave his sister a peck on the cheek before leaving the room. "I'm gonna get into town. I need to pick up a few things. I'll catch you later."

"Hold on," Josie piped up just as he reached the hallway. Ben came back, poking his head around the kitchen door. "Are *you* bringing someone? To the dinner party, I mean?"

Ben looked over at his brother, giving him a sly grin. "Nah. I think it'd be better to keep our minds focused on business, don't you, Ade? Or were you dying to introduce your latest girl to the family?"

Aiden felt a jolt in his stomach then he shook his head. "Nope. You're right, bro. It's a business dinner."

"Great." Josie looked satisfied then she scribbled something in her diary as the front door slammed.

"I'd best go see to the horses," Greg said, then he stood up. He kissed Josie fondly on the top of her head. "Don't you go overdoing it, ya hear?"

She giggled but gave him a dazzling smile when he left

the room.

"I'm glad I've got you to myself," she confided to Aiden as she started to clear away the pots. "What's this about a girl? Is it anyone I know?"

Aiden grimaced. "Actually, I was going to talk to you about her." He got up and helped with the dishes. "I know Ben wouldn't approve of her, but I was kinda hoping you might."

She stared at him, intrigued. "Go on."

"It's this girl I really like but we're not exactly going out. Well, we went out last night but…"

"But? Did you have fun?" Her eyes sparkled with curiosity.

"Yeah, we had a great time." He sighed when he remembered how it had gone. It had been great right up until…

"So she's obviously real nice. Why the long face, bro?"

"She's a waitress," he explained.

"And?" Josie was clearly unperturbed.

"Well, she doesn't have much money. I took her to Sebastian's last night without thinking. I was afraid she was going to refuse to go in at first, but she was okay in the end. In fact, she acted like she belonged there. She knew all about the wine, said she's actually been to France. We had a real good time." He smiled, remembering their meal together.

"But?" Josie frowned. "What happened, Ade?"

She could read him like a book. He huffed.

"I took her home. Josie, you wouldn't believe how that poor girl lives. The place is cold and drafty, and she hasn't got any decent furniture or carpets or anything. I felt so —"

"Guilty?" Josie put her arms around her brother.

He nodded. "I didn't want her to feel uncomfortable with me there. I tried not to look shocked or anything, but I ended up upsetting her."

She pulled back from him sharply. "How? What did you say?"

He went on to explain about the book and their conversation, while his sister winced.

"I don't know why I said it. I was only joking."

"I can see why she was upset." Josie nodded at him slowly.

He sighed again. "I know."

"Sounds like she's a proud woman, even if she doesn't have much," Josie went on thoughtfully.

"She's that all right. Had a bit of a fight on my hands when it came to paying the tab. She wanted to go Dutch on it." He shook his head, remembering how that had gone.

"Hmm, it must be hard for her," Josie remarked.

"I want to help her, sis. I just don't know how." He felt a knot in his stomach at the hopelessness of the situation.

"Maybe we could ask her to come help with the dinner party? She obviously knows her stuff, and we could pay her really well? It would help us both out. Think she'd want to?" Josie's eyes shone as she looked up at her brother.

He frowned. "I don't know." He chewed his lip.

"Well it'd be a bit classier than that café she's working in, I'd imagine, so it might give her a bit of a boost in morale as well as wages," she suggested, "and Lord knows I could use all the help I can get."

"You've got a good point there." He suddenly felt a little better. "I'll talk to her about it once I've made my peace over this mess," he said decisively. "Thanks for that, sis." He bent down and gave her an affectionate kiss on the cheek before grabbing his hat on his way out the door. At last something seemed to be working out.

* * * *

Aiden grinned as he climbed into his truck and made for the little café in Bracken Ridge. He knew Maggie wouldn't be looking forward to seeing him today, but he had to do *something*.

He was right. She scowled at him from the counter when he went in carrying a large bunch of flowers. He was expecting it, though, and shot her a dazzling smile. Although she was deliberately keeping busy serving another table, he took his usual seat at the counter and waited for her.

Eventually she came over to him.

"Morning, Maggie. I've brought you these."

She shook her head. "I don't want them. I don't want anything from you. In fact, I'd rather you left right now and never came back. Think you could manage that?" Her face was tight and her tone as cold as ice.

He shook his head. "Nope."

She huffed, folding her arms as she stared at him defiantly.

He knew she was hardly likely to make a scene with other customers there, but deep down he was worried that she really wanted him to go.

She narrowed her eyes. "What do you want from me?"

"A coffee and one of your delicious cinnamon buns, please." He grinned, hoping to see her thaw a little.

She didn't.

She pursed her lips angrily then looked over at the other customers. He was obviously right about her not wanting a scene. She poured him a drink and handed him the warm bun. It smelled delicious.

He smiled and took the plate but was surprised when she didn't let go. Instead, she leaned into him and spoke through gritted teeth in a low voice.

"And I'd be obliged if you'd leave the correct amount on the counter. I don't need your massive tips. I don't need *anything* from you."

She let go of the plate so suddenly he almost fell backward off his stool. His heart sank. He stared up at her, but instead of standing there chatting with him like she usually did, she stalked off and went to wipe down some tables. *Shit!*

Chapter Four

Maggie felt sick to her stomach as she busied herself wiping down all the tables in the little café. She scrubbed at the plastic tablecloths until they were all shiny then took a jug of water to top off the small bunch of wild flowers that she'd placed in the middle of each one.

Aiden was still sitting at the counter when she'd finished, so she decided to wash the windows next—anything to avoid having to speak to him. With any luck, he would take the hint and leave.

Her throat was sore where she had been crying most of the night, and she knew she didn't look her best. Bags had appeared under her eyes, and her skin looked sallow with tiredness. She'd hardly slept a wink, which she knew was ludicrous. They had only gone out together once, but it had been a perfect evening, until the end. She hadn't realized just how much she liked him until she'd thrown him out of her home. He'd seemed really genuine and hadn't even looked shocked when he'd seen the state of her apartment. But when she thought about it, everything added up. He'd taken pity on her and given her big tips every day that he'd been in here, his subtle way of giving her money. He'd flirted with her, made her believe he was interested in her before asking her out. Clever. Then he'd purposely taken her to a swanky restaurant after telling her that they'd just be going for a drink, maybe a bar meal. He was clearly trying to make her feel uncomfortable and out of her depth. Well, he could damn well think again if he thought she was about to make a fool of herself. She smirked as she recalled their conversation about the wine, then remembered how he had assumed afterward that it had all come from a book. *That guy knows nothing.*

"Could I get another coffee in here?" Aiden asked when she went behind the counter to fetch a bucket of clean water for the windows.

His big blue eyes looked watery and sad, and he sure wasn't smiling now.

"Sure." She took the pot over and refilled his cup.

He put his large, warm hand over hers as she went to move away, and she turned back in surprise.

"Maggie, I'm so sorry about last night." His voice was low and gentle.

She shook her head. "Don't sweat it. I'm really not that bothered."

The hurt in his eyes was palpable, and she felt like a prize bitch, but there was no way she was going to let him know how much he had crushed her. She'd stupidly thought there was something between them, but all along he'd been making fun of her, showing her up for the pauper she was. *Well, a fat lot he knows.*

"Please, Maggie. Let me explain." He held her hand tightly as she went to pull away, and she quickly looked around to see if any of the other customers were watching. They weren't.

"There's nothing to explain, Aiden. I've got your measure." Her teeth were gritted again as she fought back the tears that threatened her eyes. Her throat felt heavy, and the large lump that had formed there last night seemed to be settled in for the week.

"I didn't mean to insult you," he told her firmly.

"Then, why did you?" She glared at him, finding it easier to show her anger than her hurt.

"I was joking. That's all. I know you know your stuff. Hell, that's one of the things I love about you. You were such fun to be with last night, and I wanted to see you again. I *want* to see you again." He'd corrected himself before she'd even taken in his words. She was still hung up on the '*that's one of the things I love about you'* line.

His eyes were pleading with her to believe him, and she sighed as she watched a couple leave the café.

"You think you're better than me, don't you?" she snapped.

He shook his head. "No, I don't."

"You thought I'd be embarrassed in that restaurant, that I'd make a fool of myself. You were hoping I would be out of my depth, use the wrong knife and fork or something. You were shocked as hell that I knew about the damn wine. I'll bet that ruined your night. "

"You're wrong." He shook his head again.

"And you insisted on paying the bill because you thought I wouldn't be able to afford it, didn't you? You even took me home just so you could turn your nose up at my apartment. Well, Mr. Smart-Ass, you've had your fun. But you know what? I don't care. I've got more class in my little finger than you'll ever have, so don't you think you're better than me 'cause you're damn well not." She spat the words out at him, narrowing her eyes as she tried to stop the tears from falling from them.

She failed. Quickly turning away so he couldn't see her cry, she yanked her hand from his grip and fled into the little kitchen. It afforded her no privacy as it was surrounded by glass, enabling her to cook and watch the café at the same time, but she slammed the door and leaned back on it just the same.

She took a tissue from her apron pocket and quickly blew her nose before wiping her face. Aware that she was being watched, she went over to the sink and washed her hands, carefully dried them on a small towel, then looked through the window into the café. She was surprised to see that the last of the customers had gone, leaving their money on the table, and Aiden was the only person in there now, still perched at the counter.

She seethed. Had their scene just turned away her customers? If so, Mr. Burton had better not hear about it, or she would definitely be out of a job. She opened the door and walked toward the counter where Aiden was sipping his coffee.

"If I lose my job I'll know who to thank," she told him vehemently.

He smacked his lips together noisily. "If you lose your job, I'm sure you'll find a better one. Lord knows, you're qualified enough."

It wasn't the answer she was expecting, and it floored her somewhat.

He raised his eyebrows at her lack of response. "Well, you *are* a lot more than just a waitress and cook in a small café, aren't you?" He went on. "Anyone with half an eye can see you don't belong here. You're a lot better than all this." He waved a hand, gesturing their surroundings.

She felt more than a little taken aback. He was right. She was much more than just a waitress in a crummy café.

"How... How do you know?" Her voice was much quieter than she'd intended, but she was still trying to squeeze it out past that massive lump in her throat.

"It's obvious, Maggie." He shook his head with a smile. "You're right about having class. That's exactly what you've got — and, yeah, a darn sight more than I'll ever have."

"I didn't mean..." She suddenly felt embarrassed for her tirade. He was a Fielding, after all.

"No, I mean it. Class is something you can't learn. You've either got it or you haven't, and you've got it by the bucketful." He smiled at her. "I can't tell you how sorry I am for the way things ended last night, darlin'. I had such a great time with you. I didn't want it to end at all, let alone like that. I-I'm an idiot. I know that."

Her heart melted as he spoke, and she took a step closer to him.

"No, *I'm* sorry. I should have realized you were only joking. I overreacted. I'm afraid I've got a tendency to do that. I'm a bit too sensitive for my own good." The lump in her throat begin to thaw as the knot in her stomach slowly unfurled.

Suddenly Aiden was around the back of the counter, taking her in his warm arms, and his lips encased hers in the hottest kiss she'd ever had. His cologne enveloped her in a haze of happiness, and her whole body began to relax for the first time in years. Her pussy ached when his hard erection dug into her, and their kiss intensified. She ran her hands through his soft fair hair as she lost herself in the depths of his big blue eyes.

They both jerked apart when someone came in the door, and she stood blushing as Aiden grinned then made his way back around the counter.

"All right, darlin'?" He winked at her and he took his hat. She nodded, a big smile spread across her face.

"Good. Don't forget to put those in water, now, will ya?" He indicated the large bouquet of beautiful flowers he had placed on the counter.

"Thank you." She lifted them up. The sweet scent surrounded her.

He nodded and headed for the door just as the other couple took their seats by the window. The smirks on the customers' faces told her they'd seen the kiss, but Maggie didn't mind. She was proud that such a handsome guy had wanted to kiss her. *And* it looked as though he wanted to see her again.

She popped into the kitchen and filled a large jug with cold water before placing the flowers in. She placed them on the counter where they looked lovely. Now she could stand and admire them all day, remembering the gorgeous cowboy who had given them to her.

* * * *

It was a quiet day in the small café, and Maggie spent most of it cleaning. She was aware that most of the jobs didn't really need doing, but she was eager to pass the time in the best way she could.

As she swept under one of the window tables, she noticed a newspaper that had been left on the sill by one of the customers. The daily paper was a luxury she couldn't afford right now, so she was pleased to see that it was current, and she put it aside until she stopped for a coffee break.

A few minutes later, she came to a stopping point. She stretched as she hopped onto one of the stools at the counter and poured herself a warm drink. There had been no customers for over an hour, and she was sure the place would have to close down soon. *Perhaps I could find another job in here?* She spread the paper over the counter and started to read about the shenanigans and events of the local community.

An article caught her eye, and she felt herself go stone cold. *Oh no!* There was a photograph of a happy couple and a lengthy article about the man's success. It appeared that a certain Robert Rossington had recently become engaged to a local lady, Lorraine Parry, and was planning some big changes for his fiancée's large estate.

Maggie shook her head as the article waxed lyrical about the wealthy businessman and his benevolent nature, painting him as some kind of hero who deserved to be worshiped for his many charitable endeavors.

But he wasn't a hero. He was a bully — and a thief. Maggie knew it, although she could never prove it. She closed her eyes as his voice invaded her thoughts, informing her that one of his contacts had discovered that the manager of her bank was about to be investigated for fraud.

They had been living in a large house in the country, which, although it was mortgaged to the hilt, served as a status symbol for Robert and a millstone for Maggie. He employed a housekeeper to enable her to spend more time writing, following the success of her first book, *A Modern Guide to Social Etiquette*. It appeared that many of the landed gentry had worked their way into their wealth and had little idea of what was expected of them in the social circles of the upper echelons. Those born into money had such niceties bred into them as part of their education, but the 'new rich' were at a loss.

Her book had soared, having already provided her with a large advance and nice royalties, which had led to her being invited to give talks on the subject at many of the ladies' groups and society meetings in and around the local area. Maggie had become something of a celebrity and had even appeared on a daytime television program, which again saw a massive rise in sales of her book and in her presentations. Discretion was one of the most important parts of her new career, and she was often asked to help the nouveau riche on a one-to-one basis, hiding their embarrassment and ignorance, while netting her a small fortune.

Her fiancé of eighteen months suddenly had become famous by association, and he'd used his new position to his advantage—borrowing money and influencing decisions purely based on his name, or, rather, hers.

He'd begun mixing with people whom Maggie would rather he avoid, and he'd soon fallen into a gambling habit that he could never break in a month of Sundays. Of course, she had been unaware of the severity of his problem until it was far too late.

On his insistence, she'd withdrawn all her money from the bank, fearful of losing it to a potentially fraudulent manager, and she'd hidden it all in the safe in Robert's study. It hadn't been there more than a couple of days when she'd arrived home from a book-signing event to be told that they had been burgled and every cent was gone. The sheriff had been less than helpful, and she'd known she would never see her money again. The evasive attitude of the so-called investigating officers had roused her suspicions about the whole situation, but it hadn't been until Robert's activities had come to light that she'd finally realized the truth.

Having run up horrendous debts, her fiancé had taken to gambling his way out of trouble. It might have worked had he been a more skillful poker player, but he had lost everything they owned—and a lot more besides. To dull the pain of his loss, he would drink himself into a stupor, aided and abetted by his new 'friends' who, of course, had been only too happy to join him in running up his tab at the local bar.

Maggie's promotional work and seminars had used up most of her time, and she had been unable to pen another book, although it had always been her intention. Oblivious to the problems at home, she had begun to donate a large portion of her earnings to local charities — a gesture for which Robert had taken all the credit, unbeknown to her at the time.

Her efforts to discuss financial matters with him seemed to increase his fury, and one night he rewarded her tenacity with a black eye. It wasn't just her fiancé that had hit her that night. The truth had, too.

Chapter Five

"Did you ask her?" Josie whispered while she cleared the plates from the supper table.

"Not yet. I wanted to give her some space, you know? I mean, we only just made up." Aiden shrugged as he followed her over to the sink with more dishes.

"Is this about the mystery woman?" Ben taunted when he came up behind Aiden, making him jump.

"She's not a mystery." Aiden pouted.

"Then come on, bro. Spill the beans. Who is she?"

"Never you mind." Aiden brushed past his older brother and finished clearing the table.

Ben chuckled. "I'll find out sooner or later," he promised him, giving Josie a quick kiss on the cheek.

Aiden glared at him, knowing it was true. He could never keep a secret from Ben for long.

"What time's Greg due back?" Ben asked their sister when he picked up his hat.

"About another hour or so, I guess. I've got his supper ready to reheat as soon as he calls to say he's on his way." Josie wiped her hands in a thick towel.

"Well, you just take it easy," Ben warned her with a wink as he left.

"I will." She grinned.

"I hope this dinner party isn't going to be too much for you." Aiden frowned, suddenly remembering that their sister was pregnant. "You have plenty people to help, haven't you?"

"Yes, of course. The caterers will deal with all the food, and I've hired some help to wait on us all. And there'll be

Maggie, of course. I thought she could be in charge of 'front of house' duties. What do you think?"

"Sounds good. I just hope she's free." Aiden had begun to wonder if asking her on the day of the party wouldn't be too short notice for her, but he really hadn't felt that it was right to talk about it earlier.

"Hmm." Josie nodded thoughtfully. "It would be good to have her take a look over the table and everything just to make sure it's all perfect before the guests arrive. Then she can help greet them and take their coats. We'll have drinks in the front room. If it's not too cold, I thought we'd open up the French windows so we can go out onto the decking if we want to."

Aiden nodded. "Great. It'll be good to have plenty of space to talk business with the guy if the opportunity arises."

"Give me a call in the morning. Let me know what she says." Josie followed her brother to the door. "Goodnight."

Aiden bent down and gave his sister a kiss on the top of her head. "Night, sis. Shout up if you need anything."

She smiled then he left her to go to his own house, which was just a short way down the drive.

* * * *

Maggie felt a shiver run down her back as she left her apartment in the darkness of the dawn. It was sure getting toward winter, but it wasn't just the chill in the air that made her feel uncomfortable. Although there was no one in the quiet backstreet, she felt as though she was being watched...again!

Shaking her head with a self-deprecating sigh, she told herself it was just her imagination. She often had feelings like this, more so in the past few weeks, though. *Probably Aiden's comment about the lack of lighting around here putting me a little on edge.*

Bracken Ridge was a small, sleepy village and right now most of the townspeople were sleeping, she reminded herself. Pulling her well-worn coat tighter around her, she quickened her pace a bit and headed for the café.

Once she had the coffee pot on and the smell of fresh bread wafting from the oven, she felt a lot better. The flowers on the counter looked stunning, the roses already emerging from their tight buds. She smiled. Aiden Fielding sure was a handsome guy, and she was flattered that he would pay so much attention to her. Being only a year or two older than her, she wouldn't normally consider any kind of relationship with him, but the guy actually seemed older than his years. She was impressed that he was planning to expand the ranch, and the idea of riding lessons around here was a really good one. No one else was offering them. The Fieldings were going places, and that's just where *she* wanted to be, too.

"Morning, beautiful."

As though some magic spell had brought him straight from her thoughts into the café, Aiden was suddenly standing in front of her.

"Aiden." She gasped in surprise, not having even heard him come in.

He wore a dazzling smile that she couldn't help but reciprocate.

"It's early." She frowned. "I haven't even got the cinnamon buns in the oven yet."

"That's fine. I can manage without them just this once," he told her with a surreptitious smile.

She eyed him curiously. "Is everything all right?" She wedged open the kitchen door so they could talk while she put the food to cook.

"Yeah, fine. Mind if I help myself to coffee?" He was already on his feet and around the counter.

"Sure. Sorry, I should have —"

"No, no. You're busy. I can see that. Besides, you're right. I *am* a little early. You can't be expected to do all your preparation *and* serve me." He grinned as he took the pot and poured himself a cup. "You want one?"

"Yes, please." She switched on the timer and joined him behind the counter.

"Here." He handed her a cup, and she smirked at the irony of *him* serving *her*.

"Haven't we got this the wrong way around?"

He chuckled. "I think, after all the running around you do for everyone else, it's about time someone waited on you for a change."

She smiled, taking a sip of her coffee. "I like the sound of that," she told him.

"Good." He winked at her then went back to the other side of the counter where he took his usual seat.

"The flowers are beautiful," she said, nodding toward the jug on the counter.

He smiled. "You're real good at arranging them."

She laughed. "I didn't have to do much, although, actually, I have qualifications in flower arranging."

He grinned. "I was kind of hoping you might say that."

She raised her eyebrows, relieved that he hadn't thought she was boasting.

"My sister's throwing a dinner party tonight, and I wondered if you'd like to come along? Between you and me, she's a bit out of practice with these things and could use a little help and guidance, if you wouldn't mind?" He looked sheepish, and she stared at him in surprise.

"Me?"

"Yeah. It's nothing too fancy but it's an important event — well, to the family, anyhow. Thing is… Josie's pregnant, and we don't want her getting all stressed about stuff, so I just wondered if you'd —"

"I'd love to!" She beamed. It had been years since she had been invited to any kind of formal event.

"You sure? You wouldn't think —?"

"I wouldn't think anything. I'll look forward to it. What time should I be there? I don't finish here until six tonight, I'm afraid." She chewed her lip as her mind raced. She knew it was early days for her and Aiden, but this sure was a step in the right direction if they were going to try any kind of relationship, as she'd hoped. It was endearing of him to be a bit coy about asking her over to the family spread, and she guessed he must be nervous about introducing her to his kinfolk.

He frowned, seemingly a little surprised. Had he thought she would read too much into it? Was he afraid that she would think he was moving too fast? He needn't worry. She was quite happy to take things slowly.

He pursed his lips thoughtfully. "We've arranged for guests to arrive from eight o' clock with dinner being served at nine, so really, as soon as you can get there would be great."

"Don't worry. I won't let you down," she promised as a young couple entered the café.

"I know. You're great, Maggie. I really appreciate this."

"I'm real glad you asked me." She smiled.

"What time should I pick you up? Shall we swap cell numbers?"

Maggie reached for a napkin and hurriedly scribbled her contact number down for him, secretly amused at his subtle way of asking for it. "Call me, and I'll save yours," she told him, smiling.

"Great. Thanks, darlin'." He tucked the napkin into his pocket then grabbed his hat before leaning over the counter to give her a quick peck on the cheek.

Maggie felt herself go hot. She watched the handsome hunk leave the café before turning her attention to her customers. Today just wasn't going to go fast enough.

* * * *

Having spent all day deciding what to wear for her date, Maggie rushed home to prepare as soon as her shift ended. It had been a long time since she had been invited anywhere as prestigious as a dinner party, and she couldn't wait. After a quick shower, she dried and styled her hair into a sleek updo with plenty of pins and some diamante clasps. Her makeup took a little longer than she had expected, and she had only just finished when her cell rang.

The unknown number could only be one person, and she felt a warm glow as she answered it.

"Maggie? It's Aiden."

That was what she'd hoped. "Is everything okay?" She couldn't help noticing some concern in his voice and, for a horrid second, thought he was going to tell her he'd changed his mind about taking her tonight.

"I've just been delayed a while, darlin'. Nothing to worry about. I'm still in Almondine sorting out some business. I've arranged a cab to pick you up and take you over to the ranch, and I'll meet you there. Is that okay with you?"

Her body relaxed. "That's real thoughtful of you, Aiden. You didn't have to do that."

"I'm real sorry to let you down, sweetheart, especially as you're doing us such a favor and all. I just didn't want to get you there any later than you had to be."

Her heart melted. *Me doing him a favor?* He clearly had no idea how much it meant to her that he had asked her to accompany him tonight.

"It's fine, Aiden, honestly. I'm almost ready anyhow," she assured him.

"Well, that's good. The cab should be there for you in about ten minutes. Is that okay?"

Maggie gasped. He sure wanted her to get there on time. In fact, she was concerned that she would be the first to arrive at this rate.

"That's great. I'll see you soon."

"Thanks, darlin'. I look forward to it."

She beamed as she placed the cell back on the dressing table. Her best evening dress was hanging on the outside of the wardrobe where she had put it. Admiring it as she put on her underwear and nylons, she let her mind drift to the last time she had had a chance to wear it. It had been a few years ago, and she and Robert had hosted a party for some important clients of his. He had bought her the dress especially, and she'd felt really good in it, although slightly self-conscious. Her hand trailed over the sparkly material as she took it down and began to put it on. When she had first tried it, she had balked at the amount of cleavage she'd had on show, and she had been surprised that he hadn't told her to change. She had felt sexy in the dress, right up until he'd said it might help his case if the guests were too busy gawping at her tits to read the contracts properly. Robert had a way of ruining things.

He wasn't going to ruin tonight, though. She was sure Aiden would appreciate her body in the dress, although she had a small wrap just in case it was a bit inappropriate in front of his family.

She stood up straight while she pulled the zipper up the side, shocked at how much tighter it was than she remembered. She winced as she peered at her reflection, disappointed at how large she looked, but there was no time to change now. She could already hear the cab beeping down in the street.

"I'll just be a minute," she called out of the open window, and the driver gave her a wave.

Maggie stole a couple more minutes to double-check her hair and makeup, then she took her silver purse and slipped her cell into it. One more glance in the hallway mirror on her way out convinced her that, if nothing else, the midnight blue of the dress complemented her eyes perfectly, and she cautiously made her way downstairs. It had been a while since she'd worn heels and the dirty, sticky, steps were totally at odds with her cocktail dress and strappy sandals.

On the way to the party, she saved Aiden's number into her contact list and sent him a quick text to say she was on her way. As she typed an X at the end, she felt like a horde of butterflies was racing through her stomach.

"Here we are," the driver told her as he pulled in at the foot of the steps that led to the main ranch house.

"Thank you." She delved into her purse.

"All paid for, miss," he told her when he got out to open her door.

"Oh."

A Strauss waltz was playing while she carefully made her way up the steps, and she could hear laughter from inside the house. Taking a deep breath to steady her nerves, she looked up as someone opened the door.

"Hello." The guy was just a few years older than her and looked a little surprised to see her. He was very handsome, though, and wore a smart black tuxedo with gold cufflinks.

"I'm Maggie Welch," she informed him with a smile.

He looked slightly amused as he stood back to allow her in. "Welcome, Maggie. I'm Ben Fielding."

"Aiden's brother? How nice to meet you." She smiled politely and held out her hand, which he shook while displaying a rather bemused expression.

"Can I take your wrap?" he asked kindly.

"Um, no. I'll hold onto it for a while. Thank you," she answered, pulling it a little tighter around her when she saw his eyes flit over her ample bosom.

He frowned slightly, clearly puzzled, and she wondered just how much Aiden had told his family about her.

"I think Josie's in the kitchen, which is just through there," he said, gesturing down the hall.

She looked in the direction he indicated, wondering if he was suggesting she should go look for her. *This family clearly doesn't have much idea of etiquette.*

"I'm afraid the guest of honor arrived right on time," Ben muttered to her under his breath.

"Oh." She had only arrived a few minutes late. Fashionably late, she would have thought, and felt it odd of him to mention it.

A passing waiter swept through the large hallway with a tray of drinks, and Maggie was horrified when Ben took one for himself then proceeded to sip it as the guy walked away. Seemingly oblivious to her expression, Ben ushered her in the direction of the kitchen. They had only taken a few steps when a pretty young girl in a waitress's outfit rushed up the hall toward them.

"Oh, Theresa, this is Maggie," Ben said.

The girl looked surprised. "Oh, right. Josie's been waiting for you. She wants you to help with the canapés," Theresa told her, looking confused.

"Oh, of course." She turned to Ben, who looked anxious. "It's okay. Your brother mentioned that she might need some guidance," she confided in a low murmur.

Ben grinned, visibly relaxing a little. "Oh, that's all right then. I'd begun to wonder if —"

"Ben, there you are!"

Maggie felt her blood run cold as a familiar voice boomed up the hallway, and they all turned around to see Robert Rossington walking toward them with a slim, beautiful lady in tow.

"Robert, I'm sorry, I was just…" Ben looked a bit flustered.

"Margaret?" Robert stared at her in disbelief, his eyes wasting no time in finding her breasts.

She pulled the shawl tighter, noting his line of sight with a shudder. Robert was even more portly than she remembered, and he sported a mustache that looked far too thin for his round, pockmarked face. His ginger hair was receding, and he had a bald patch showing right on top of his head, which Maggie guessed probably continued around the back.

Aiden's voice behind her made her turn suddenly, and she was shocked to see a pretty woman in a black dress carrying a tray of canapés walking beside him.

"Maggie?" His voice sounded almost strangled, and he stared at her in amazement.

"Oh, *you're* Maggie. I've got the…" The woman offered her the tray then quickly pulled them back, looking quizzically at Aiden.

"I thought she was supposed to be helping," Theresa huffed.

"Well, yes, but…" The woman with Aiden stared

uncomfortably from Maggie to Aiden, and he squirmed.

"Helping? You mean as in...*serving*?" Robert couldn't contain his mirth.

"Yes, but..." the woman stuttered again, nodding slowly.

"I don't understand. Who is this woman?" Robert's partner frowned in bemusement, pointing at Maggie, who felt herself go hot, inside and out. To make matters worse, Robert's partner was tall and elegant, with perfect bone structure and white-blonde hair fastened in a beautiful chignon with curly tendrils framing her gorgeous face.

"She's supposed to be the hired help, and yet here she is, dressed up like a dog's dinner—a *cheap* dog's dinner at that!" Robert guffawed.

Tears began to well in Maggie's eyes as she realized her mistake, and she stared, horrified, at Aiden. He was just gaping at her, mortified.

"Oh, no." Ben looked slightly amused as he looked from Maggie to Robert, who was now practically rolling about in hysterics.

Maggie felt the tears begin to trickle down her face, and she bolted for the front door as quickly as she could in her heels.

"Maggie," she heard Aiden calling after her, but she slammed the door behind her and fled.

She didn't stop running until she was a good way from the ranch. She wanted to call a cab to take her home but she didn't have a signal for her cell, so she removed her heels and walked along the grass verge, trying to recall the route the taxi had taken just a short while ago.

Despite the warmth of the evening, she couldn't escape the freezing shivers that racked her body or the constant stream of tears that blurred her vision as she stumbled miserably in the growing darkness.

Chapter Six

Aiden stared at the front door that Maggie had just swung shut behind her.

"I should go after her."

"No, you shouldn't. In the kitchen, now!" Josie spoke through gritted teeth, ushering him back down the hall.

He could hear his brother join in the laughter with their guests and Aiden seethed, hoping Ben was just trying to schmooze them.

"What the hell did you say to her when you asked her to come?" Josie demanded, her eyes fiery and accusatory.

Aiden frowned. "Surely you don't think I—?"

"*Exactly* what did you say?"

He racked his brain. "I just said we were having a dinner party, and would she like to come along? And that you needed some help with it." As far as he could recall, that was as much as he'd said.

Josie stared at him in disbelief. *"We're having a dinner party, and would she like to come?"* She would certainly have shouted had they not had company. Her face was bright red and she looked like she could kill her brother.

"And the bit about needing help," he added quickly. "I didn't just invite her to join us."

"Well, you obviously didn't make it clear." She was mad as hell.

"I don't understand." He scraped his hands through his hair, messing up the neat style he had perfected earlier.

"Well, that's makes two of you," she said to him. "The poor girl didn't understand either, and now look what's happened."

"Yeah, I think maybe I should just go after her and explain—"

"You will not! We've got a party to host, in case you've forgotten. You'll have to ring her later. Give her time to calm down first. Now you just get out there and see to the guests. Jeez, they must think we've totally abandoned them."

Aiden was more concerned about Maggie thinking he'd abandoned *her*. How the hell would she get home? Did she even know where the ranch was?

"Now," Josie insisted.

He huffed but did as she said. She was probably right about Maggie needing time to calm down anyhow. The way she had stood staring at him while that damn Rossington guy laughed at her had made his heart melt. *Why didn't I say something?* He couldn't believe he'd just stood there gawping back at her.

He'd been taken aback by how beautiful she looked. She was definitely a classy lady, which was apparent in the way she held herself. She sure looked sensual in that dress, too. How the hell Rossington could call her cheap was beyond belief. He was really beginning to hate their guest of honor, and Aiden doubted whether all this upset was worth the land, after all.

"There you are, bro." Ben's voice was casual as he greeted him back in the living room, although the look in his eyes was a giveaway to the tension he was feeling.

"Sorry. I was just helping Josie out," he told his brother, giving him a forced smile.

"Yeah, well it looks like Margaret isn't much of a help, is she?" Rossington sniggered, much to the surprise of his partner.

Aiden felt his blood boil again, and he tensed up immediately.

"Lorraine was just saying how eager they are to take a vacation," Ben interjected quickly. "They've just got to sort out this business with the land then they're going to the Mediterranean for a few weeks."

Aiden bit his lip hard, looking over at the woman.

"Did you say the Mediterranean?" Sylvia Crowthorne, one of their other guests joined them, smiling.

"That's right," Lorraine stated with a smug expression.

"How lovely. I've been there a few times. Glorious weather." Sylvia was an old hand at schmoozing clients, which was why Ben had invited her and her husband, Frank, along.

"Yes," Lorraine replied noncommittally.

The drinks were coming thick and fast, and by the time they sat down to eat, Rossington was already slurring his words. "So, how do you know Margaret?" he asked as the soup arrived.

That was exactly what Aiden had been desperate to ask *him* ever since that debacle in the hallway, but he had thought better of it.

"She's local," he replied airily. "How about you?"

Rossington sat forward on his chair. "Well, actually it's a long story," he said, as though he was about to reveal the mystery of the Sphinx.

Sylvia cleared her throat, making them all look up. *Damn.* Aiden was keen for the guy to continue, but the look on Sylvia's face told him it might not be appropriate dinner-table talk. He had to concede she was right, although it was a great pity.

"So, how quickly will you have all this land-business wrapped up?" Sylvia asked, breaking a small piece of bread from her roll. "Your fiancée looks anxious for that holiday." She winked conspiratorially at Lorraine, who actually smiled back at her.

"Well now, that all depends," Rossington pontificated, clearly enjoying his moment in the spotlight.

"I should imagine it would be pretty straightforward," Frank said to him. "As long as you have all the paperwork in place to verify that you own the land and the buyer can prove that he has the funds to pay for it, it should be done and dusted in a matter of hours." Being a retired lawyer put him in the ideal position to comment on the subject.

"Ah, well…" Rossington suddenly looked uncomfortable and hastily took a rather large sip of his drink.

All eyes were suddenly on him as everyone stopped eating and stared at him curiously.

"You *do* own the land, I presume?" Sylvia asked jovially, before letting out a polite laugh.

"Well, not exactly on paper," Rossington spoke slowly, his face turning quite red. Aiden wondered if it was the guy's conscience or his alcohol consumption that was responsible for his ruddy complexion.

"It's in *my* name," Lorraine piped up, matter-of-factly.

Aiden frowned. "Why is that?"

"It was a condition of Daddy's will," she told them. "All his assets were to stay in the family until they were legally sold. When Robert inquired about changing the deeds over to his name, the attorney said he couldn't do that unless we were married. That's when Robert had this great idea to become engaged. Well, it would have happened sooner or later, wouldn't it, dear?"

Lorraine's big doe-eyes would have been endearing had the situation not been so tragic. The look on Rossington's face told them all that it was obviously the *only* reason for the engagement. The drunken fool didn't even try to hide it. He gave her a wry smile that didn't meet his eyes, and he continued to slop the soup down his front.

"So, have you named the day?" Josie asked politely.

"Well…no, not really. Robert's so busy with work and everything. He hasn't really had time to discuss it properly, have you, dear?" Lorraine turned to him for affirmation again, but shook her head resignedly when she saw he was totally absorbed in trying to pry a chunk off his bread roll.

Aiden spent the rest of the meal watching their honored guest get drunker and hearing him become more vocal.

"Why don't we sit on the terrace with our coffees?" Josie suggested as their dessert dishes were cleared away.

Despite the time of year, it was quite stifling in the dining room, and Aiden noticed that his pregnant sister looked flushed.

"What a good idea," Sylvia agreed, rising to her feet.

Aiden watched everyone but Rossington get up and make their way toward the door.

"Perhaps you'd prefer to stay here and have some cognac instead?" he offered graciously, well aware that his guest was probably incapable of standing up right now.

Ben shot him a puzzled frown when he followed the others out, and Aiden winked at him as he took the decanter from the small side table.

"I can see you're the clever one in the family," Rossington growled, taking his glass. His chunky fingers cradled the brandy balloon rather clumsily, and Aiden knew he wasn't as used to all the airs and graces as he pretended.

He nodded politely and took a sip of his own drink, sure that the drunkard had no idea *just* how clever he was.

"So, how did you meet Maggie...er, Margaret?" Aiden asked once his guest had sat back comfortably in his chair.

"Ah." Rossington looked around the empty room conspiratorially. "Well now, that's a bit of a funny story, actually."

Aiden leaned forward.

"Well now, I notice she's calling herself Maggie Welch these days, but when we were together she was still Margaret Shepperton-Welch."

Aiden frowned. He'd seen that name somewhere but couldn't quite place it. "Sounds very grand," he mused.

"I'd say. D'you know the Shepperton-Welches? From Penkridge Manor over at Almondine?"

Aiden frowned. "Well, yes of course, but—"

"Disowned her, they did. Probably why she's changed her name." Rossington sniffed as he took another sip of brandy.

"But why?" Aiden's mind reeled at the realization that Maggie was actually part of the richest family in Cavern County.

"Ah, well," Rossington said smugly, "*I* might have had something to do with that." He chuckled.

Aiden seethed but waited eagerly for him to continue.

"I've never much liked working for a living," the older man confided, "so when I saw her picture in the local rag, I thought I'd try my luck. She was doing some charity thing or other, so I tracked her down. I know she's not much to look at but she was mighty rich back then."

"When was this?"

"Oh, a couple of years or so. Ha! Don't let on to Lorraine, though, will ya? Don't want her figuring out my little game, you know?" He had now started waving his finger around much like an old-fashioned schoolmaster.

"Your game?" Aiden was angry yet intrigued.

"Yep. Love 'em and relieve 'em," he said with a snigger.

"You mean love 'em and *leave* 'em?" Aiden corrected him.

"No!" Anger flashed in Rossington's eyes, taking Aiden by surprise. "I know what I mean."

For a second it looked as though his guest would happily have struck him in his fury, but it soon dissipated and the older man chuckled again.

Aiden said nothing, but he took another small sip of his drink as he waited for the guy to continue.

"Actually, when I say 'love' what I mean is '*make* love'. You know, *fuck*." He chortled. "Then I relieve them of their money. I love money." He gave a satisfied nod, and Aiden guessed he was thinking about a pile of cash.

"And how do you do that?" Aiden tried not to sound too inquisitive, but he had to know.

"From their family. Rich families are always happy to treat each other, so I just become part of that family." He sounded quite matter-of-fact, and Aiden knew he had long since forgotten who he was talking to.

"So you marry them, these women?"

Rossington looked horrified. "Good God, man, not if I can help it. Nearly had to with Margaret when the family stopped coughing up, mind you. Looked like the only way to get any more out of the tight-fisted lot! I always wondered if they'd cottoned on to what I was up to. That mother of hers is a shrewd woman, believe me. Anyhow, then Margaret hit the jackpot with some book she was writing. Sold millions, it did. Got a hefty advance on it, too—probably 'cause of who she was. Still, the cow kept it all locked up in the bank so I couldn't get my hands on it. So I came up with some bullshit about her bank manager and got her to withdraw it all. While she was away, I lifted the cash and gave some of it to the local sheriff—or law enforcement officer, or whatever he called himself—who was only too happy to help cover my back, if you catch my drift?" He burst out laughing. "She wasn't so dumb, though. No, just like her mother." He grimaced. "Thought I'd got away with it at first, but the dang woman became suspicious once she'd got over the shock. Accused me of robbing her, she did! Me! Well, I just saw red, as you can imagine."

"You... You struck her?" The words almost stuck in Aiden's throat.

"You could say that."

Rossington looked a little thoughtful, and Aiden wondered if he actually regretted his actions.

Then he let out a chuckle, which answered Aiden's question for him. "Went around to that old battle-ax of a mother, she did. Thing was, I'd got there first. While she'd been away, I'd visited the old bag and told her I was worried about Maggie. That she'd taken to telling the most awful lies lately."

Aiden narrowed his eyes incredulously. "So you turned her family against her, then when she went around there for help because you'd hit her, they didn't want to know?" His blood boiled.

Rossington gave him a massive grin. "Yup. Clever, eh? I still keep in touch with them now. You never know when that sort'll come in handy. Might be good for a decent wedding present, if nothing else!"

"Are you for real?" Aiden shouted as he shot to his feet.

Rossington looked up at him in astonishment.

"Aiden, we need you out here." Ben was suddenly at the door, calling him over with a face like thunder.

When Aiden didn't respond, his brother marched over to him and practically hauled him out of the room.

"Sylvia and Frank have to leave now. Say goodnight." Ben was talking through clenched teeth, and Aiden just stared blankly at him, not quite understanding the situation.

He opened his mouth but Ben spoke first. "*Now*, bro."

Their guests were standing in the hall, having put on their overcoats.

"Thank you for a wonderful evening," Sylvia said as they exchanged air kisses. "Calm down," she whispered into his ear.

"Thank you," Aiden replied before shaking Frank's hand.

"I've called a cab for Lorraine and Robert," Josie said as they waved to the elderly couple. "Should be here any minute."

"Can he walk?" Lorraine slurred slightly from behind them.

They all turned around to see her clinging to the doorframe of the living room.

"I don't think *you* can," Ben told her, swooping over to lift her into his arms. "Come on. Let's get you inside." He carried her back into the lounge and laid her on the sofa, smiling.

"The cab's here," Josie called from the front door.

Aiden turned to fetch Rossington, but Josie stopped him. "*I'll* get him," she insisted.

"No, *I* will. Aiden, you take Lorraine." Ben's deep voice called to them, and Aiden did as he was told.

"Who are you?" Rossington looked totally bemused as Ben practically dragged him from the dining room. He glanced around the hallway at the family as though they were all total strangers.

"He won't remember any of this in the morning," Lorraine

told them as Aiden helped her into the cab.

Aiden sighed. At least there was *one* good thing about tonight, then.

Chapter Seven

Maggie hated working on Sundays. And the thought of having to smile and be nice to people today made her stomach churn.

After a hot shower — which did very little to relieve the aches in her legs and soreness of her feet — she pulled on a pair of jeans and big, comfy sweater. Her eyes were baggy and red where she had cried most of the night instead of sleeping, and her whole face sagged with fatigue. She swiped a bit of mascara across her lashes and a whisper of gloss on her lips then dragged a comb through her hair.

"Don't tell me you're against me this morning, too," she growled angrily at her wayward curls. She grabbed them together in a tight band before twisting them up into a bun. She had hoped for a neat, severe look to match her mood, but her hair had other ideas, as it dropped down and hung in casual strands around her face.

"Great!" She rolled her eyes at her reflection before deciding she couldn't be bothered to mess with her looks any longer. "You'll do," she told herself, then threw on a thick jacket.

It was cold and windy when she started to make her way toward the café. A shudder ran down her back as she heard footsteps behind her, and she chanced a look around. Straining to see in the darkness of the late autumn morning, she was bemused to find the street deserted. She had definitely heard something, but it had stopped now. A little unnerved, she continued walking but didn't notice any noise after that, and, once she hit the main road, the sounds of traffic and the wind drowned out any footsteps.

The wind always made her feel agitated, so she was in no better mood by the time she arrived at work. She followed her usual routine of putting on the coffee pot and warming the oven, then she pulled up the blinds and opened the café.

The sneering expression of Robert Rossington and the sound of his cruel laughter had haunted her all night. The dumbstruck face of Aiden Fielding staring at her in disbelief kept flashing through her mind. How could she have been so stupid? Why would she think that Aiden would invite her to dinner with him and his family just because they had been out once? Why in hell did it have to happen in front of her ex, of all people? She took out her temper on the bread dough as she kneaded and pummeled it to within an inch of its life.

"Morning, Maggie."

She stilled when a familiar voice called to her from the counter. After taking a deep breath, she turned to face Aiden, who was standing, anxiously staring through the doorway at her.

"If you think I'm going to wait on you hand and foot, you can damn well think again." Her teeth were gritted and her voice vicious. "I refuse to serve you, Aiden Fielding. You are *not* my superior, no matter what you might think, and I'd thank you to leave these premises right now." Her voice rose while she strode out to the counter and pointed to the door.

His face was pale, and he looked tired and worried. "I need to talk to you," he said. "It's really important."

"Nothing you can say to me is important because *you're* not important," she responded vehemently. "Now get out before I call the sheriff!" Her blood boiled as she yelled at him.

"Maggie, I need to—"

"You need to get out of here!"

"I'm sorry about last night, but—"

"I don't want to hear it. Just go!"

"But—"

"Now!" She leaned over the counter toward him, and they were almost nose-to-nose as she hollered at him. His scent surrounded her, and she could see how much he was pleading with her, but it didn't matter. It *couldn't* matter. He'd made a damn fool of her, and there was no apology in this world that could make up for that.

Aiden huffed, fiddling with the hat in his hand, but he could obviously see his efforts to reason with her were futile. His lips were pursed tightly when he finally stalked back over to the door. Without a backward glance, he was gone.

Hot tears trickled down Maggie's face and she quickly swiped a hand over her eyes while she headed back for the kitchen. Her breathing was heavy as she tried to steel herself, but as soon as the scent of baking bread replaced Aiden's favorite aftershave, she crumpled and sobbed heavily into her handkerchief. Her stomach ached as much as her heart, and she felt as though she were about to faint.

She sat on the little stool, weeping uncontrollably for several minutes before she finally conceded that she really was not fit for work today.

"Two coffees when you're ready." Damn. A couple of guys had just walked in and plunked themselves at the counter, one of them in the seat which Aiden usually took.

Quickly splashing cold water onto her face, she turned and went out to serve them.

"You okay?"

Both guys looked taken aback by her appearance as she dried her face in her handkerchief while pouring coffees with the other.

"Yeah. Just a bad cold, I think," she said to them, forcing herself to smile.

"You should be home in bed," the second guy piped up.

Her head shot up angrily, expecting to see a salacious grin on the older man's face, but she was surprised to be met with a sympathetic frown. She nodded, grateful for his kindness. "I'm thinking of ringing my boss and taking the rest of the day off," she shared.

"You should," he replied.

"Thanks." The younger guy smiled as she handed them their drinks.

She quickly dived into the ladies' bathroom to check on her face, which, as she had feared, was red, puffy and devoid of what precious little makeup she had used this morning.

"Oh, God!" She splashed more cold water into her eyes but it wasn't doing much good, she had to admit.

When she went back into the café, she was surprised to see that quite a few more customers had arrived and were all sitting around chatting. Quickly she went over to serve them, only too aware that she hardly looked presentable enough to be doing her job, though no one seemed to notice her.

After that, there seemed little point in calling the boss to ring in sick. She had already worked half her shift before she even had time to sit down, let alone make the call.

* * * *

Aiden seethed as he gunned the engine and sped back to the ranch. He knew Maggie would be sore with him today, but he hadn't expected to not be able to speak to her *at all*. That woman sure had a fiery temper on her, though he couldn't really blame her. How could he have been so stupid?

"I should have gone after her last night," he said to his sister when he joined her for coffee a short while later. "Now she won't even talk to me. Hell, I don't even know how she got home from here."

Josie sighed. "And you really think she'd have wanted to talk last night? Aiden, she's a woman, not a child. She's perfectly capable of getting a cab home if she wanted to. Besides, you were needed here, in case you'd forgotten?"

"Yeah, and what a waste of time that turned out to be,"

he groaned.

"We heard you yelling at the guest of honor," she told him with a grimace. "Let's hope he was too drunk to recall that."

"You wouldn't believe what a lying little shit the guy is!" Aiden felt his blood boil as he remembered their conversation in the dining room.

"Who? Rossington?" Ben arrived just then, throwing his hat and gloves onto the chair next to his brother before plunking himself at the table opposite him. "Any coffee left in that pot, sis?"

Josie nodded, standing up to pour him a cup. "Yeah."

"Doesn't even own the dang spread." Ben chuckled incredulously. "Good thing I asked Frank and Sylvia along. We wouldn't have thought of bringing up the subject without them. I just assumed —"

"We all did. Why wouldn't we? I mean, some guy says he's selling a piece of land. You don't generally ask him if he actually *owns* it, do you?" Aiden shook his head. "The whole night was a damn waste of time, if you ask me!"

"Not necessarily," Josie piped up. "After all, you're in a much stronger position now than you were this time yesterday. You now know that Rossington doesn't own the land. I'll bet he doesn't want many people knowing that. And you know it belongs to Lorraine, so *she's* the one you really need to schmooze."

Aiden stared up at her as the cogs whirred in his brain.

"She's right, bro. I'd say last night was a good little fact-finding mission, if nothing else." Ben nodded, taking another sip of his coffee.

"And I know all about that shit with him and Maggie," Aiden added thoughtfully.

"Is that what all the hollering was about?" Ben asked.

"Yeah. He stole from her. Came right out and admitted it."

"Is that a fact?" Ben looked up in surprise.

"Knock, knock," a man's voice called from the hallway.

"Come on in, Frank," Josie shouted, standing up to fetch another coffee cup.

"Well now, it looks like I arrived at just the right time," the older man said, spying them all sitting around the kitchen table drinking coffee.

"You sure did. Any news?" Josie placed a cup of the strong, black liquid in front of him as he took his seat next to Ben.

Aiden looked up, frowning.

"She's not looking too good, I'm afraid," Frank replied, taking a sip of his drink. "Said she was planning to go home, but, by the time we left, the place was getting mighty busy. I guess she'll have to stay there now."

"Maggie?" Aiden narrowed his eyes, having noticed the conspiratorial looks Josie was giving the old man.

"Yeah. I felt really bad about letting her go like that last night, so I asked Frank to check in on her today. You did say she was at the café opposite the Melrose in Bracken Ridge?" Josie looked a little sheepish.

Aiden nodded.

"It was on my way. Had to give my neighbor a lift into town anyhow," Frank assured them.

Aiden sighed. "She was real upset when I left her," he admitted ruefully.

Frank nodded. "She seems like a strong woman. I'll bet she'll bounce right back up again before you know it."

Aiden wasn't so sure. Maggie Welch might look like she was tough and wouldn't let anyone hurt her, but he suspected otherwise. That woman had been treated real badly in the past, by all accounts, and she must be fed up of picking herself back off the floor by now.

"Rossington was her ex," he told them. "He admitted to me last night that he stole every penny she had and turned her whole family against her."

Josie stared at him, tears welling in her eyes. "Oh, no." She put her hand to her mouth. "No wonder she was mortified last night when he saw her in the hall."

Aiden nodded. "Great timing, eh?"

Frank frowned. "He admitted it?"

"Yes, sir. When we were sipping brandy last night. Of course, he didn't know I knew Maggie, not that he was sober enough to care about that, anyhow."

"Sounds like he's planning to do the same to the lovely Lorraine," Ben mused.

"Yeah, that girl sure seemed clueless about him," Josie agreed. "Seems to dote on the money-grabbing bastard."

"She's not the brightest star in the sky, is she?" Ben added thoughtfully. "Though there's something about her..."

"What exactly did he say, son?" Frank asked Aiden, who was only too eager to relay the whole, sad story.

"Think there's anything you can do, Frank?" Josie asked, wide-eyed when they had finished talking.

He turned to her with a nod. "It's possible. It was only a couple of years ago, so everything should be pretty accessible, and I'm pretty sure the guy in the sheriff's office over at Almondine is the same guy who's been there for years. I can get some questions asked—surreptitiously, of course—and get a couple of my pals in the attorney's office to do a little digging. If Maggie spoke to the sheriff about it, it should have been documented. I'll be interested to see how deeply they managed to bury this one—if at all."

"You think there's actually going to be a record of the burglary?" Aiden frowned.

"There might be *something* pertaining to a burglary at the premises, just to make it look authentic." The old man nodded. "A load of baloney, of course, but something we can use all the same."

Aiden felt a lurch in his stomach as a grain of hope reared its optimistic head. He knew Maggie Welch didn't want any help from him right now, but she was going to get it anyway.

Chapter Eight

Maggie couldn't remember a day when she had felt so relieved to finish work and begin the walk home in the cold evening air. She had forced herself to keep working today, despite her early morning 'wobble'. Although she had kept half an eye on the door all day in case Aiden came back, she hadn't seen anything of him, although she had received yet another message on her cell telling her how sorry he was. Yeah, right. He'd left plenty of those texts last night and had tried ringing her umpteen times, but she had switched her phone to silent mode and thrown it in a drawer as soon as she'd gotten home.

The fact was that he saw her as a subservient. He hadn't invited her to dinner. He'd invited her to *serve him* dinner — him and all his toffee-nosed friends, including Robert fucking Rossington. What in hell was a guy like Aiden Fielding doing rubbing shoulders with the likes of her ex, anyway?

She was still seething when she rounded the corner into her little back street. Her fury had made her walk much faster than she would have normally, and she was pleased to notice it was still light enough to see when she got home. Pulling out her key, she jumped when she heard footsteps behind her.

"Don't make a sound."

She'd know his voice anywhere. It had plagued her nightmares for the past couple of years. The fact that it was accompanied by a strong stench of stale whiskey filled her with even more dread.

Her fingers trembled as she fumbled to turn the lock, silently praying for one of the neighbors to come to her rescue, but they were alone.

"W-What do you want?" she demanded as he pushed her through her own front door, causing her to sprawl across the thin hall carpet.

The door slammed behind them.

"So, this is what the place is like on the inside," he sneered, switching on a light and taking a good look around. "I often wondered."

Maggie clung to the wall where she pulled herself up, watching him lock the door behind himself then tuck the key into his pocket. *Bastard*. Her blood ran cold. "Y-you've been watching me?" It all made sense now, the footsteps, the feeling of being followed... It hadn't been her imagination after all.

"I wanted to find out what you were up to these days," he told her nonchalantly as he finally pulled his hand back out of his pocket.

"Up to?" She spat the words at him as he crossed the hall and took a peek into her tiny kitchen. "I haven't been up to anything. I work for a living—good, honest work, something you know nothing about."

He reached her with one stride, and pure evil stared back at her as she watched him raise his hand to strike her.

"Don't you fucking dare!" Anger and indignation pooled with fear as she screamed at him.

"Or what?" He narrowed his eyes when he grabbed hold of her upper arms, pinning her roughly back against the wall. "You planning on stopping me, bitch?"

"You— You're hurting me," she wailed as he squeezed her soft flesh.

"So? It's nothing to what I'll do if I hear you've been making trouble for me. D'ya hear?" His voice was a feral growl and his teeth were gritted.

Pain seared through her arms. She struggled to free

herself from his grip, but it was no use.

She shook her head. "Trouble? How?"

He stared into her face before pushing her one more time into the wall behind her and letting go of her as though she burned his fingers.

"What in hell were you doing at the Fielding Ranch last night?" he demanded.

She felt herself go hot when she recalled the scene in the hallway. "You know damn well. I was asked to *work* there," she snapped.

He let out a hideous guffaw. "Is that why you were dressed up in that awful dress? The one *I* bought for you?"

"With *my* money!" she added.

She half expected him to yell at her again—hit her even—but he just burst out laughing. It was a taunting laugh, hollow and ugly.

"I chose it," he told her matter-of-factly. "It showed a good bit of cleavage, which, in those days, was nice to look at."

She felt an ache deep within her as she considered what he was saying. Had he tried to make her look stupid, or did he think it would impress his friends to see her dressed like that? Until last night she hadn't thought it too revealing, but perhaps with the extra weight she had gained, her breasts had made the dress sag a little more than she'd imagined. Had she really looked awful each time she had worn the dress, including last night?

"Fuck you!" she yelled at him, fuming that he had managed, yet again, to make her doubt herself.

"You wish!" he taunted her. "I've got a much younger, slimmer model to fuck these days, or hadn't you noticed? One with a lot more money than you ever had."

"It didn't stop you fleecing my family, though, did it?" she snapped.

This time she didn't see his hand coming. It swiftly flew through the air and planted a loud slap across her cheek.

"Ah!" She tasted the iron tang of blood on her lip when

she reeled backward, bumping her head hard against the wall as she slid down to her knees.

"Your family was only too happy to offload you onto me, and you know it, bitch," he snarled vehemently. "They couldn't wait to get rid of you."

"That's a lie!" she protested, her head pounding.

"Is that why they welcomed you back with open arms when you went crying home to Mommy, then?" His teeth were tightly clenched again, and she noticed that his fists were, too.

Bad memories that had never been far from her mind swamped her aching head, and misery engulfed her once again. Although desperate to stop him from tormenting her, she thought it would be better not to retaliate. She'd never been sure just how much he was capable of and she really didn't want to find out right now. Instead, she just gawped up at him, awaiting his next move with dread. He was standing over her so she couldn't get up, and she knew he had the advantage. *Best not to antagonize him any further.*

They stared at each other in silence for a few more minutes. Then her phone suddenly hummed as it vibrated in her purse, and he looked around for it.

"Who's that?" he demanded.

"How should I know?" She rolled her eyes at him before realizing what she was doing and prepared herself for another blow. With her eyes screwed shut, she felt her heart pounding as hard as her head, but he didn't hit her. Instead, she heard him take a step past her and she opened her eyes to see him rifling through her purse.

She quickly stood up and took a step away from the wall. She'd read somewhere that it was always best not to have your back to the wall when being attacked, and, right now, she was definitely being attacked. He stared incredulously at the screen. "Aiden? As in Fielding?" He looked up at her, frowning. "Why's he calling you?"

"M-Maybe he wants to offer me more work," she stammered, thinking quickly.

The way he narrowed his eyes at her made her even more nervous.

"You haven't got a thing going with your boss, have you? Is that why you were all tarted up like a Christmas tree last night? To impress him?" His voice was smarmy, and much as she would love to wipe the sneer from his face, she couldn't risk him knowing her business, especially if he was doing some kind of deal with the Fieldings.

"Ha. As if!" She forced herself to scoff as she pulled a face.

"He didn't look too happy last night." He narrowed his eyes again, seemingly unconvinced.

"Yeah, right. That'll be why he came running after me to take me home, I suppose?" She sneered, her mouth going dry.

He looked thoughtful for a second. "True," he conceded, "and, let's face it, he's way out of your league nowadays, isn't he?"

She licked blood from her lip as she forced herself to say nothing. Her whole body shook with a painful mixture of fear and anger.

Robert let out another derisive guffaw. "You won't be doing any more work for them, do you hear? You'll stay well away from the Fieldings from now on."

She stared up at him in disbelief. She recalled his patronizing tone from when they had been together, and she'd hated it then, almost as much as she did now. *How dare he?*

Although every fiber of her being willed her to tell him exactly what she thought of his audacity, the cruel glint in his eye reminded her precisely what the consequences would be. It wasn't worth it. *He* wasn't worth it.

"I wasn't planning on it anyway," she mumbled.

"Good." He sneered, evidently satisfied that she was complying with his wishes, clearly oblivious that she was just stating a fact.

With a grimace, he seemed to have difficulty pulling the key from his pocket as he headed back up her tiny hallway.

Eventually he yanked it out, swung the front door open and threw the key across the hall. Giving a gloating snort, he glared at her once more before striding out.

It wasn't until she heard the large door at the bottom of the stairs slam shut behind him that she dared to move, quickly rushing over to shut the cold draft from the apartment — to shut him out! She leaned back against the door then slid down into a heap on the floor, weeping uncontrollably at the helplessness of her situation. She wasn't safe. She knew that. The pain in her face was already causing her head to ache even more, and the burn in her arms seared through her body. It was nothing, however, compared with the agony that ripped through her heart.

* * * *

Aiden was reeling with the events of the day. He and Frank had taken a trip to the local sheriff's office where Dyson Shearer informed them that the sheriff at Almondine hadn't changed in the past ten years.

"I don't know him all that well," Dyson explained to them. "Seems to keep himself to himself quite a bit, if you know what I mean. Not the friendliest of guys, either, if I'm honest, but maybe that's just me."

"No, I can imagine," Frank responded. "Can you do me a favor and look up a matter he would have dealt with a couple of years ago over there? I just need a case number at this stage."

Dyson nodded. "Of course, Frank. What's it all about?"

They sat around the wooden desk and explained the whole story to him, and he frowned as he checked out the details on his computer. "If it's been reported, it'll be on here," the deputy explained. "All the computers in Cavern County are linked up. That way we can tell if a job is connected to another one nearby or whatever."

"So you'll be able to get any intel on the incident?" Aiden's heart was in his mouth as they stared at the whirring screen.

"Yup. Whatever was reported and what happened about it. Mind you, this information's all confidential, you understand? I can't just go and—"

"We understand that, son," Frank assured him with a pacifying gesture of his hand. "We don't want to get you into any trouble. We just want the case number so we can verify first-off that it was definitely reported. We'll take it from there."

"Can't you ask the lady in question? I mean, if she went to the cops to ask for some kind of verification that this Rossington guy had actually reported a robbery, they would have given her the case number." Dyson frowned.

"She doesn't know we're here," Aiden blurted out.

Dyson looked up in surprise.

"What we mean is… We don't want to go dragging up bad memories for her if we don't have to," Frank interjected. "If the case is genuine, then we'll follow it up, but if the case was never even filed, we're looking at a whole different ball game."

"Have you got a date or an address where this took place?" Dyson asked doubtfully.

"Nope," Aiden said him with a grimace.

"It's going to take some time to track down a burglary without the details," Dyson warned them, sighing.

"I know, son. But it's not impossible, though, eh?" The older guy winked at Aiden.

Dyson chuckled. "Well, Frank, I can always rely on you to keep me busy in this job," he told him. "Let me run a few reports to see what I can come up with. The fact that we've got the victim's name should help, and that it was Rossington who reported it. Why don't you guys go grab a coffee down the road, and I'll shout as soon as I find something?"

"You're a good man, Sheriff," Frank said as they got up to go.

"Yeah, and I'll be an old one before I get to the bottom of this, no doubt," Dyson sniggered.

Chapter Nine

"How was she when you saw her?" Aiden asked as he and Frank sat down in the small diner. He couldn't help wishing they were back at Bracken Ridge right now. Even the coffee tasted better over there.

Frank sighed. "I'm not gonna lie to you, son. She didn't look good."

Aiden's heart sank a little deeper.

"She was sobbing her heart out when we got there. Didn't notice us at first," Frank went on. "Said she had a cold or something, but we knew that wasn't the case. Pretty girl, too." He took a sip of his coffee.

"Yeah, I think so." Aiden's gut wrenched as he thought of Maggie's soft curves and that beautiful face. "I really like her, you know?"

"Yeah, I see that," the older guy confirmed. "Judging by how upset she was, I'd say she likes you, too."

"I don't think she does right now," Aiden told him ruefully. "I've really hurt her, you know, Frank?"

"Yeah, I know, son."

"I went back to her place. It was damp. You could see it on the walls. Makes me wonder how people can actually charge rent for places like that." He seethed as he thought about it.

"So what happened? Josie said you asked her to come do some work for you last night?" Frank looked at him curiously as he took another sip of his drink.

"Josie and I thought we'd found a way to give her some extra money without it looking like a handout," Aiden answered him, and he went on to explain the whole debacle.

"Ouch." Frank winced when he'd finished. "I can see that must have hurt."

"It wasn't supposed to. I couldn't just give her money. No way would she accept it." Aiden knew it sounded feeble. "But she really knows her stuff, Frank. She wrote this book on social niceties — you know, how to entertain guests and things like that. Even how to fold a napkin. I took a look on the Internet. It sold millions."

"Hmm, that's why Rossington stayed with her, I suppose," Frank mused.

"What I don't get is, why did *she* stay with *him*?" Aiden took a sip of his drink as he shook his head.

"Maybe she didn't think she had a choice," Frank offered. "Has he got some kind of a hold over her?" He frowned.

Aiden was sick to the pit of his stomach. "God, I hope not." The thought hadn't occurred to him before. "I don't know. She didn't say, but then, she wouldn't." He was sure of that. Maggie Welch was a proud woman and wasn't about to start telling folk about her problems. Heck, she hadn't even told him what Rossington had done to her.

Frank shook his head. "No, I don't suppose she would," he replied thoughtfully.

They both looked up as Sheriff Shearer strolled over to their table. "Well, it's not great news, but it's not all bad either," he said as he sat down. "The incident was recorded as a burglary, but it seems no fingerprints were found at the scene. It went down as unsolved."

"Well, at least that's something." Frank's optimism was a great relief to Aiden, who had immediately feared the worst.

"So what exactly does that mean?" Aiden hardly dared ask.

"It means that, according to the county records, there *was* a burglary committed at the premises, but there's not much to go on by way of evidence." Dyson frowned, deep in thought.

"So we can legally look into the case and make inquiries

about what was done — or not done — about it. If it turns out the police officers were negligent in their investigations, Maggie will have the right to sue. Either way, Maggie — or her legal representatives — can take action for misconduct," Frank explained.

Aiden's heart surged a little. It seemed there was hope, and right now that was all he could wish for.

"The investigating officer was a guy named Campbell Taylor," Dyson told them. "Not the friendliest of folk, if I remember correctly, but he's been on the job a long time."

Frank stood up and shook the sheriff's hand. "We'll be careful," he replied with a smile.

* * * *

Almondine was a real busy town, not like Pelican's Heath. This place was much bigger and the volume of traffic running up and down the main street made Aiden's head spin. He certainly hadn't expected it to be this rammed on a Sunday. Everyone seemed to be rushing about all over the place, and there wasn't a friendly face in sight.

"What are we gonna do, Frank?" He frowned as he watched the old man take in the scene before them. They were both being jostled by the busy townsfolk as they stood on the sidewalk contemplating their next move.

"We're just on a fact-finding mission for now, son. Don't mention anything about Maggie or the missing money. Let's just see what this guy's really like." Frank looked toward the sheriff's office then his eyes fixed on a small diner not far from it. "Looks like a good place to start," he muttered, half to himself.

Aiden followed him over. He could see he was certainly going to get his fill of coffee today.

The diner was busy and rowdy, but not in a good way. It wasn't friendly chatter like they were used to back home. These folks all seemed grouchy about something or other, not least the time it took to get a cup of coffee.

"You harvesting the coffee beans yourself, Ellen?" a scruffy-looking dude moaned over the counter as the guys stood in line.

"I've only got one pair of hands, Seth Painter, and you well know it!" The older lady was pouring out some drinks and grimaced at the sarcastic remark.

After that, the woman proceeded to slam down every pot and cup she was using, clearly irked by her customers' attitudes, which did nothing to welcome the strangers into town.

"Good day, ma'am. I'd like two cups of coffee when you're ready, please." Frank tipped his hat and smiled at the woman who stared back at him, agog.

"Coming right up." She seemed amazed at having a well-mannered customer and clearly wasn't used to being spoken to so politely.

"Thank you kindly, ma'am." Frank tipped his hat again as he took the tray from her and turned to where Aiden indicated a vacant table.

"I sure am glad I don't live here," Aiden confided once they were comfortably sitting by the window with their drinks.

Frank snickered. "I think it takes a certain type of person to live in a hectic place like this," he agreed.

They spent a short while soaking in the unpleasant atmosphere. The air was heavy with smoke, and it seemed that Ellen had burned some toast earlier. The food that was carried through from the steamy kitchen looked grease-laden and totally unappetizing, and most of the customers were complaining and groaning about the service — or lack of it. The poor waitress was rushed off her feet, flustered and bad-tempered, and Ellen wasn't much happier.

A large guy in a deputy's uniform grabbed Aiden's attention when he pushed his way right to the front of the line, demanding today's special. The other customers seemed resigned to his lack of manners, and Aiden guessed this must be normal behavior for the sweaty dude.

"I'll be sitting over here." The guy indicated a table next to where the men were sitting, and they watched in horror as a young girl quickly vacated the table for him, despite not having finished her meal.

Aiden caught Frank's eye and noticed that he was also watching the guy with interest, but they said nothing.

"Any news on my stolen horse, Deputy?" A portly man in an ill-fitting business suit approached him as he stared out of the window. The deputy didn't even glance up. "I'm on lunch!" he snarled, and the businessman scurried away, muttering a hasty apology.

When the waitress arrived with his meal, the guy only managed a grunt of acknowledgment as he tore his eyes from the street and picked up his fork.

Something told Aiden that this had to be the man they were searching for, and he continued to watch surreptitiously as the guy gobbled down his lunch. His clothes seemed starched and crisp, but his sandy-colored hair was lank and hung in thin strands around his shoulders. His face wore a constant sneer as he occasionally glanced around the diner, mentally daring anyone to interrupt his break. His eyes were small and mean-looking, and thick gingerish stubble peppered his chin. The atmosphere seemed even more uncomfortable and edgy while the guy sat there, and Aiden noted how many people left the diner. The room became much quieter and even Ellen seemed a little more careful with the dishes, although no less sullen in her expression.

Aiden quickly finished his coffee as he caught Frank's indication that they should leave, and he stood up to follow him out. On their way past the counter, Frank dropped a bill in the jar and was rewarded with a surprised smile from Ellen as she wiped down the coffee machine.

"Excuse me, ma'am." Frank leaned over the counter to speak quietly to her. "Is that guy the local law enforcer around here?" He cocked his head in the direction of the scruffy dude, and Aiden watched the woman's face fall into a disparaging leer.

"Yup, that's Deputy Taylor," she confirmed with a nod. "He's all we've got, I'm afraid, but don't expect too much from him." She rolled her eyes, and Frank chuckled.

"That's kinda what I thought. Thank you, ma'am." Frank gave her a conspiratorial grin and tipped his hat politely. The woman afforded him an appreciative smile as they left.

* * * *

"One of the horses has escaped from the bottom field," Ben told him when Aiden eventually got back to work.

He frowned. "How in hell did that happen?" He was already pulling on his gloves as he followed his brother toward the stables.

"I've no idea. Jeremy's already checked the fence. It's all secure. Gate was still bolted, too."

"Any sign of the horse?" They each mounted and set off toward the south of the ranch.

"Jeremy thinks it must have gone over onto Rossington's land — or, rather, Parry's." Ben didn't look happy.

"Let's hope he doesn't notice. Frank reckons he might not have even sobered up yet."

Ben frowned. "He sure put away a few drinks last night."

"Probably more like a few bottles, if anyone was counting." Aiden shook his head.

Jeremy met them at the gate to the south field. It housed twenty-five thoroughbreds, twenty-four of which were grazing happily in the half-light of the setting sun. "Looks like we're okay, boss. Sam and Ashley have caught up with the horse. They're bringing him back now."

Aiden felt a surge of relief. The last thing he wanted was to spend the night searching for a horse, and he wasn't too sure how amenable Rossington would be to them riding over his land — or, at least, *Parry* land.

"Did it get far?" Ben looked relieved, too.

"Seems it had gone a fair few miles," Jeremy told them.

"Damn! It had to be Rossington's land, of all places." Ben

grimaced.

"You sure everything's secure here?" Aiden couldn't help wondering if it was just coincidence.

"Yup. I've no idea how it got out," Jeremy said, frowning. "I double-checked the fences myself. I can't find any damage or rotten wood."

"Let me just triple check," Aiden offered as he dismounted.

The foreman was totally right. There was no sign of any damage or wear on any of the fence panels, and the gate was secure and intact.

"Have the veterinarian check out the horse as soon as they get it back here," Ben instructed when Aiden returned empty-handed.

"Yes sir."

"You suspect foul play?" Aiden muttered as they headed back.

"I dunno." His brother pursed his lips thoughtfully. "But something sure doesn't add up around here."

Chapter Ten

Monday mornings were always tough, but waking up on her hallway floor with a crick in her neck and the mother of all headaches reminded Maggie that they didn't come much worse.

She groaned as she stood up slowly, stretching the kinks from her back, using the wall for support. She was surprised to have fallen asleep, given that Robert had left her lights on, and she wondered whether she had actually passed out instead.

She went to the bedroom and flicked on the lamp, glad that it was still quite dark outside. As she plunked herself on the side of her bed, she glanced over to the dressing-table mirror and gasped. The left side of her face was bright red and a purple bruise was already beginning to swell over her cheekbone, giving the appearance of a black eye. *Damn.* She could hardly go to work looking like this.

Stripping off her clothes, she climbed into the shower. As usual, the water wasn't very hot, but she felt much fresher after a good wash, and she examined the bruises on the rest of her body while she was waiting for the conditioner to tame her unruly hair. She must have fallen quite hard onto the floor when he'd pushed her in through the front door, as she had what appeared to be carpet burns on her stomach where her top had ridden up. There was also a large bruise appearing on her chin, and her arms and legs were riddled with purple marks. Robert Rossington had sure done some damage.

Angry tears flooded her face, which she turned up to the streaming water. She winced as the coldness hit her bruises and quickly finished her hair before stepping out then wrapping herself in a large towel. Her body longed for the huge, soft, fluffy towels she used to have when she was with Robert, as her sore skin was chafed by the rough, threadbare ones she had only just managed to afford.

She stared at her tired, swollen face in the mirror and felt like crying all over again. How had she come to this?

"Okay, Maggie. There's only one thing to do," she told herself. "You've got to pull yourself up by the bootstraps and get on with it." It was a conversation she'd had quite a few times over the past couple of years, and it never seemed to get any easier. Usually it was an unpaid bill that got her down, but this was the lowest she had ever gotten. Not only was she broke, she was also in danger. She knew she hadn't seen the last of Robert Rossington.

She applied a thick layer of concealer to her cheek before covering her face in foundation. It didn't really hide the bruising, but it made her feel a bit more confident about her look. Then she applied the rest of her makeup, a touch heavier than she usually wore, but she wanted to balance her look as much as she could.

It was nearly ten o'clock by the time she arrived at the café. She had walked quickly enough but turned around each time she'd heard someone behind her, half-expecting to see Robert again. She had never opened so late in the day, and somewhere in the back of her mind had worried that a long line would have formed around the café, with hungry diners waiting impatiently for her to appear and feed them. She smiled to herself when she saw that the street was, in fact, deserted.

She busied herself with her usual routine as she baked some fresh rolls. The smell of baking bread and hot coffee cheered her. The café was quiet for most of the day, leaving Maggie time to dwell on recent events.

The whole situation with Aiden would have been so much easier if only Robert hadn't been there to witness her mortification. Even though she was still sore at the young guy for not making it clear that he was hiring her, not dating her, it might have all blown over had Robert not been involved. Now things were so much harder, and with Robert becoming violent with her, it seemed they couldn't get much worse.

"Just a coffee, please, Miss."

A customer invaded her thoughts, and she twitched as she came back to Earth. It was an older guy who she'd seen in here before.

"Coming right up." She smiled at him and watched him balk when he saw her face.

A couple of her regulars had looked a little shocked today, though none of them had said anything and she was thankful for that.

He took a seat over by the window, and Maggie went back to idly polishing glasses. Not long after that, she heard the door open again, and she looked over to see who it was. Her stomach churned when she saw it was Aiden, and he didn't look happy.

"Maggie?" His face went white when he caught sight of her, and he stared at her across the counter.

She felt sick, and her heart thumped wildly as she struggled for something to say.

"Aiden." She kept her cool.

"What happened? Who did this?" His voice was hoarse with shock.

She quickly looked around the café. The older man was the only other customer now, but it would still be embarrassing if he overheard them. She shook her head.

"Did you call the cops? Do you know who it was?" He was clearly horrified as he walked around the counter and took hold of her arms.

"Aiden, I'm working." She indicated the man by the window, keeping her voice low.

"Don't worry about him. I'm more worried about you, darlin'. What in hell happened?" Aiden sounded a bit more frantic now, and she was surprised at just how concerned he was.

"Nothing happened. It's all dealt with. I can't talk about it," she told him, feeling his body close to hers as he studied her face.

She looked away nervously. "Aiden, just leave it."

"Like hell I will!" His voice was louder now, and she snapped her head around then stared at him in surprise.

"What?"

"Maggie, you must know how I feel about you. I'm so sorry about the other night, and I can explain. It was all a silly misunderstanding, but this is serious. I need to know who did it. Was it here? Did someone attack you on your way home?"

She shook her head.

"So, that's not why you wouldn't return my calls?" He stood behind her now as she picked up a dish towel and started to wipe over the counter.

She bit her lip nervously, hearing the hurt in his voice.

"Talk to me, Maggie," he pleaded.

"Not here, Aiden. I told you. I'm at work." She daren't turn around to face him.

"Don't mind me." The older guy slowly stood and came over to them. "I just want to help. That's all."

Maggie frowned at him as he took a seat opposite her at the counter.

"Maggie, this is Frank Crowthorne. He's a good friend of the family," Aiden told her as he walked around her to sit next to his friend.

"Oh." She nodded at Frank and managed a faint smile. He'd been in here a couple of times and had always been polite. "I didn't know you two knew each other."

"Frank's an attorney," Aiden said.

"Retired," the older man added.

She felt unnerved. "So what makes you think I need some help?" She was indignant.

"Darlin' have you looked in a mirror today?" Aiden quipped.

Anger quickly turned to despair, and she sighed. "All right. I got hit, okay? But as you can see, I'm fine now."

"I'd beg to differ," Frank told her kindly.

"Who was it?" Aiden was tenacious.

Maggie bit her lip. "I don't want you to go after him."

"I won't." Aiden shrugged.

She narrowed her eyes at him. That wasn't the answer she had expected, although she was pleased he wasn't going to wade in all guns blazing.

"Was it Rossington?" Frank asked slowly.

Maggie sighed, nodding.

Aiden's face flamed for a second, and he took a deep breath before calming himself. She was grateful that he had such good self-control. She had been half-afraid he would fly right off the handle, but he was clearly more mature than she had given him credit for. Good.

A lump hit the pit of her stomach as she recalled the bastard's threat.

"I have to stay away from you." She stared over at Aiden and her heart melted when he gazed back at her with horror in his big blue eyes.

"I think that's a good idea," Frank interjected.

Aiden's surprise matched her own, and they both frowned at the old man.

"In fact, I don't think it's a good idea that we're all here together. Anyone could come in." He got up, straightening his jacket.

"We can't just leave Maggie here on her own." Aiden looked mortified.

A cold shiver ran through Maggie, and she suddenly realized how much safer she felt with them here. Her eyes flitted to the window, and she shivered with vulnerability. She was a strong woman, though, and knew she couldn't give in to Robert's bullying. She had already traveled that route and had no intention of doing so again.

"I'll be fine," she told them, assuring herself as much as the guys. "There's a panic button under the counter wired directly to the sheriff's office, and I've got my cell." She chewed her lip a little as she blushed, knowing that she really should have called Aiden earlier.

"All right. Oh, and, it might be better if you act like you don't know me if you see me in public — or even in here." Frank looked impressed at her determination.

"What about me?" Aiden asked, standing up. "Are you saying I should stay away from her?"

Frank sighed. "I'm afraid so," he replied. "Just until we get this mess sorted out. Don't give the fuckwad any excuse to hurt Maggie any more than he already has. If it looks like she's complying with his wishes, it might be safer for her."

Maggie felt sick.

Chapter Eleven

"I just need to check on some horses." Aiden frowned once they were in the parking lot. "One of our best got out last night. They got him back, but I just want to make sure he's all right."

"How the devil did that happen?" Frank didn't look happy.

"That's what I wanna know," Aiden said. "I checked the fencing and the gate. There was no way it escaped on its own."

"I'll follow you," Frank told him with a grimace as he climbed into his own truck.

It didn't take long to reach the field where the horse had made its escape, and both men pulled over on the dirt track nearby.

"How far did it get?"

"Somewhere over there." Aiden pointed to a tree-lined field on the south side of the Fielding Ranch.

"Parry land?"

"Yup. Strange coincidence or what?" Aiden shook his head incredulously.

"Or what, I'd say." Frank scowled. "The question is... Why?"

They looked across the field where the thoroughbreds were grazing quietly.

"They seem happy enough," Frank remarked.

"Hey, boss." Jeremy walked toward them while they made their way over. "That horse was fine last night, not a scratch on him."

Aiden nodded. Ben had reported that much back to him

after the vet had left last night, but it was good to see for himself. "Any clue as to how it got out?"

The young guy shook his head when they strolled over to the gate. "Beats me."

Aiden shivered as they stood by the fence, watching the horses feeding peacefully in the field. The ground was hard and the air was cold, but it was a clear, autumn day.

"It could only have gotten out through this gate," Frank announced, strolling over to the latch.

"But who lets a horse like that loose without stealing it?" Aiden narrowed his eyes. He knew it was the only solution as to the missing horse, but it didn't add up.

Frank slowly stooped down and picked something up from the compacted mud. It looked like a tiny piece of paper that was wedged in the soil and caught against a blade of grass. He stood up, holding it up for them to see. It had writing on it.

"XS — extra small?" Jeremy frowned. "Looks like part of a label off something. My girlfriend wears that size."

Frank pursed his lips. "Could be." He rolled the paper between his finger and thumb as he pondered. It was black with gold letters and a band of gold above them. It may have had a gold band underneath the writing, too, but it was torn at a wonky angle and just a sliver of color was left. The old man carefully slipped it into his wallet.

Aiden felt a thud in his gut. "You think someone tried to take it, but it ran away?"

"If that was the case, it didn't get far," Frank mused. "Should have been easy enough to catch."

They scouted the area for any more clues, but it seemed fruitless.

"We're real careful about litter and stuff," Jeremy assured them as they kicked up the dirt in their quest.

"That's good," Frank told him with a smile. "That means this piece has to be recent. We'll take my car back."

Aiden's mind whirled as they fastened the gate again and sauntered back toward the cars. One of the hands could return Aiden's truck later. His cell hummed and showed a message from Maggie, telling him that the café was quite busy as a few of the regulars had stopped by, and that she was fine. She also told him not to worry.

Aiden felt a little easier. It was awful to think of Maggie all on her own, especially with that violent fucker on the loose. "I wish she'd let us call the sheriff," he said, half to himself as they climbed into Frank's pick-up.

"Me, too. But I can see why she won't. Domestic abuse is hard to prove, and, if she didn't report him when they were together, she's got even less of a case now. Besides, I reckon this gives us the upper hand." Frank was frowning.

"Well, I'd just like to get my hands on him." Aiden was fuming at the idea of the fucker getting away with it.

"You'll do nothing." Frank spoke firmly as he drove off. "For now, you need to carry on as if nothing's happened. You hardly know Maggie as far as Rossington's concerned, and that's what he needs to believe. Your sister just asked a local gal to come over and help out at your soiree. We don't want him knowing any more than that."

"He even told her to stay away from me." Aiden huffed angrily.

"And that's exactly what she's gonna do." Frank seemed to have it all worked out, and Aiden wished he had the old guy's patience. "You can't be seen anywhere near her. Understand?"

"But what about that crummy apartment of hers? She's not safe there. D'you reckon he knows where she lives?" He felt sick in the pit of his stomach.

Frank put up a hand in a calming gesture. "We'll find out soon enough," he assured him.

They got out of the car by the ranch house.

"Ben's here." Aiden frowned, looking over at his brother's blue pick-up.

"I need to make a quick call." Frank was checking his cell. "I'll catch up with you inside."

Aiden waved a hand in acknowledgment and headed

onto the porch. The smell of fresh bread welcomed him when he found his sister in the kitchen.

"You took your time." Ben was sitting at the large table, watching Josie lift a tray of whole grain rolls from the oven.

Aiden grimaced as he took a seat opposite his brother. "That fuckwad hit her."

Ben's eyes widened. "Fuck! So that's where he got to."

"Oh my God, is she okay?" Josie looked upset as she removed her oven gloves.

"She said she is. She's at work." Aiden's teeth were gritted. "Said there's a few of the regulars in who'll keep an eye on things."

"Well, that's good." Josie placed an arm around Aiden's shoulder, and he relished her warmth.

He managed a smile up at her. "You okay, sis?"

She nodded. "Just fine."

"Well now, that's interesting." Frank appeared in the doorway, and Josie went to the counter to fetch more cups. "Turns out the burglary *was* documented, if you can call it that."

Aiden looked up. "You managed to track it down?"

"Well, a couple of buddies in the attorney's office did, with a little help from our friendly neighborhood sheriff." He grinned. "Cam Taylor was the guy who filed it. No way of telling who did the job, though. He reckons the only fingerprints at the scene were Rossington's and Maggie's, which didn't prove anything."

"Or rather it *did*." Aiden snorted as he took a swig of the coffee Josie had just poured out. "That guy's either stupid or sly. We just need to figure out which."

"Sounds like another guy I know." Ben groaned. He glanced up at Frank. "Rossington didn't make it home last night. Lorraine reckons he was out on another bender."

Aiden felt the lump in his stomach grow even larger. "That's what *she* thinks."

"I don't think she's quite as dumb as she seems," Ben replied. "When I saw her today, she was like a totally different woman. I reckon she acts differently when he's around."

"So you've been to see her?" Frank asked, surprised.

"Yeah. I thought I should do the neighborly thing and confess that one of our horses got loose on their land," Ben said. "I was half-expecting Rossington to hit the roof, but he wasn't there. Lorraine and I had tea in their conservatory. Did you know Martha's got dementia, by the way?"

"I didn't know." Josie seemed shocked. "They always keep to themselves, so I don't know much about them. I should have made more of an effort."

"Come on, sis. We don't go nosing about in other people's business. That's all." Ben leaned forward and put a hand over hers.

Josie looked ready to cry. "I'm glad you went there today," she told him, giving him a weak smile.

"So am I. That Lorraine Parry sure is something else. And I wouldn't worry about not knowing about her mom. Lorraine wasn't told, either. Came back for her Dad's funeral to find Martha in that state. Seems the family hadn't wanted to worry her while she'd been living abroad." He shook his head. "Their own daughter."

"That must have been awful." Josie sniffed.

"Especially being next of kin," Frank interjected. "That'll be why the ranch has passed straight to her instead of Martha. Her mom won't be considered of sound mind, poor thing."

"Lorraine's determined to look after her, though," Ben said. "Sounds like Rossington mentioned putting her in a home, but Lorraine wouldn't hear of it. The guy went mental. She really thought he was going to hit her."

"Like he did to Maggie, you mean?" Aiden's thoughts were never far from the blonde beauty, but today he couldn't get her out of his head. The sight of her bruised face was almost unbearable, and he felt so guilty for not being with her now. He knew Frank was right, though. They had to bide their time instead of playing straight into

Rossington's hands.

"She's managed to get some good help for Martha and has even had the house adapted a little to make it a bit easier for her to get around. She helped Martha organize all her things to make them more accessible and she tidied out a whole lot of stuff that had been piling up in the house. She's real pleased with the results. Martha seems a lot happier, too," Ben went on as they drank their coffee.

"Well, that's good to know." Josie seemed a little relieved. "I should go around and see if there's anything I can do. Perhaps I could help with the wedding preparations?"

Ben snickered. "I wouldn't hurry on that score, sis. Lorraine's not in any rush to walk up the aisle with that dumbass."

Josie stared at him. "Really? I mean, I know they didn't seem all that close the other night, but I thought that was just because they were in company. You think she might not marry him?"

"Time will tell on that one." Ben chuckled. "Right now, I think Lorraine's more concerned with finding out what Rossington's *real* intentions are."

"He seemed pretty keen on selling off that patch of land," Aiden remarked. "You think he's faking it?"

"Oh no, he wants us to buy the field, all right. Seems he's pretty keen to sell a lot more than just that small area, though. Lorraine says he's been looking into selling off the entire spread, though he's got no idea she's found out about it."

Frank smirked as he got up to go. "Something tells me that girl's a whole lot smarter than we gave her credit for," he remarked. "Wouldn't surprise me if she's actually got her own agenda."

* * * *

Maggie took one last glance in the hallway mirror before leaving home the next morning. It had taken a ton of makeup to cover the bruise on her face, which was almost black now, but she had done her best.

As she stepped out of the building and into the street, she felt a thud of dread in her stomach. That feeling that she was being watched hadn't left her all night, and she was convinced she wasn't alone as she strutted toward the busier streets.

"Morning, Aiden." She was relieved when her cell went off and she heard his cheerful voice.

"Are you okay? Where are you?" He sounded worried.

"Yeah. I'm almost on High Street." She instinctively looked behind her. She couldn't be sure whether there was someone there, standing in the doorway of one of the derelict houses.

"Maggie?" She wasn't certain how many times Aiden had called her name, but the urgency in his voice suggested this wasn't the first.

"Yeah, yeah, I'm fine, just…" She quickened her step and breathed a sigh of relief when she reached the main street.

"Maggie? What is it? Are you okay, darlin'?" Aiden was frantic.

"Yeah, yeah… Honestly, I'm fine. I just thought for a minute that—"

"Is someone following you?"

"I'm not sure. I'm on High Street now anyhow. I haven't got far to go, and there are a few people around here, so I think it's okay." She tried to keep the tremble out of her voice in her efforts to reassure him.

"I can be there in twenty minutes, Maggie. I'll—"

"No, really, it's fine. You know what Frank said. It's best to try to act normal for a while, let the dust settle." She was almost running down the street and the café was just around the next bend. "I'm here now."

"Are you sure?"

She could already hear the quiet purr of Aiden's engine and guessed he was true to his word.

"Yes, I'm certain." She put the key in the lock and felt

herself relax a little. The familiar smell of coffee and yeast filled her senses, and she quickly got to work. "I'm here. I'm at work," she told him, trying not to pant over the phone.

"Okay. You just call me if you need me, darlin'." Aiden had obviously cut the engine, and she heard him open his car door. "I'll have my cell with me the whole time. Make sure you do, too."

"I will." She smiled, touched at his concern. He really did seem to care for her, and she felt a warm glow in her stomach that eased the lump which had settled there.

It was actually quite busy, and she was glad to be kept on her toes. She knew she'd be exhausted by tonight, though. It had sure been an eventful couple of days.

"Morning." Frank arrived toward lunchtime and plunked himself at the counter in front of her.

"Hi there." She smiled at him, remembering his advice about pretending not to know him. "What can I get you?"

"Is that donuts I can smell?" He smiled, looking toward the kitchen area.

"Sure is." She grinned. Frank was a kind man, and she wondered whether he hadn't just popped in to check up on her. Although Aiden wouldn't be coming himself in case Robert heard about it, she wouldn't have put it past him to have called Frank and asked him to stop by.

She placed a fresh donut and a cup of coffee in front of him.

Frank pulled out his wallet.

"Oh, no, it's on the house," she assured him in a whisper.

"No, no. I don't want you getting into trouble on my behalf," the old guy insisted, pulling out some cash. "Besides, if you're going to keep your job around here, you need to prove to your boss that it's a viable business. Aiden told me," he murmured conspiratorially, clearly noticing her surprised expression.

Something dropped onto the counter along with his money, and Maggie frowned at it. "What's that?"

Frank looked down in surprise and picked up the scrap

of rubbish.

"Is it yours?" She felt that sick feeling return to her stomach as she stared at the piece of paper.

"Nope. Do you know what it is?" He stared at her curiously and offered it to her.

She didn't need to touch it to know exactly what it was.

"It's from a cigar band." A vision of a particularly bad row flashed in front of her eyes. "Ever heard of Louixs?"

Frank looked stunned. "They've got to be about the most expensive smokes in the world. Who in hell uses them around here?"

"I'll give you one guess." Robert had insisted on smoking the best, even when they'd been up to their eyes in debt. Apparently it was the preferred house cigar of the Beverly Hills Cigar Club, and he figured if it was good enough for them, it was good enough for him. Not that he was, or ever had been, a member of the Beverly Hills Cigar Club, mind you. They would never have let him in!

Chapter Twelve

Maggie could almost see the cogs whirring in Frank's brain.

"Where did you get it?" She frowned.

"One of the Fieldings' thoroughbreds got out of its paddock the other night. This was in the grass just by the gate." Frank pressed his lips together tightly.

"Got out or was let out?" she asked quietly.

"That's the million-dollar question."

She could tell by the look in the old man's eyes that he already suspected the answer.

"Is it the land he's trying to sell to Aiden and his family?" Maggie pursed her lips thoughtfully.

Frank nodded.

"So there has to be a good reason why he didn't just steal the horse, if that's what he wanted. Unless... Could it be some kind of subliminal threat? Sort of, 'you'll need to buy this strip of land because next time your horses stray onto it, you'll get fined for trespassing'?" She knew only too well how Robert's mind worked.

Frank stared at her. "Of course! Ben said the guy was in a real hurry to sell. This could be his way of trying to rush through the deal."

"But why the hurry?" Maggie wiped her hands in her apron as she spoke, more out of habit than necessity.

"He doesn't own the land, so he'll either need to marry Lorraine or have her do the deal, then he'll try to wheedle the money out of her afterward. Perhaps he's nervous that she might go off the idea before he gets around to marrying her." Frank pulled out his cell and relayed their find to

Aiden.

"More coffee?" Maggie busied herself pouring another drink while Frank strolled toward the door as he spoke. It was hard, but Maggie did her best not to listen to his conversation.

Frank returned, a satisfied grin on his face. "Lorraine might not be as keen on the idea of marriage as Rossington seems to believe," he explained to her. "Ben's been talking to her, and she doesn't seem to have any kind of feelings for the guy at all. It's almost as though it's *her* that's stringing *him* along."

Maggie felt a warmth flood her stomach. "Good for her."

"We still need to figure out how he plans to get the money out of her, though." He frowned, looking thoughtful. "If they don't marry first, he'll have a job persuading her to part with all that cash."

A thud hit the bottom of Maggie's stomach. "He'll find a way." She felt her face flush as a recollection of how Robert had tried to convince her that her own money had been stolen. She had known it wasn't true, but she had no way of proving that he was lying. Even the sheriff supported his story, though she bet that must have cost Robert big time. When her mother wouldn't listen to her side of things, Maggie knew the fuckwad had won. No one was ever going to believe her. Chances were he had a similar fate planned for Lorraine Parry.

* * * *

Aiden was pleased to see Frank when he swung by the ranch a little later.

"Thought I might head on over to Almondine to see if I can dig up any more dirt on that Taylor guy. Wanna come along?" Frank grinned.

"This should be interesting," he told the older man.

"Yeah. He definitely had a hand in this business with Maggie's money. I just wondered what the state of play is between him and Rossington nowadays."

"You really think he's likely to spill?" Aiden looked over, surprised.

"I shouldn't think so, son—honor among thieves and all that. But your horse was let out by Rossington. Maggie recognized that piece of paper as part of his cigar wrapper. If I'm not mistaken, the fuckwad's about to try to cheat Lorraine Parry out of her money, the same as he did Maggie."

Aiden frowned. "You think he'd involve Cam Taylor again?"

Frank grunted. "I dunno. Sure will be interesting to find out, though."

The ride over was fairly quiet, as both men tried to avoid talk of Rossington. It didn't stop Aiden from thinking about him, though. Most of his thoughts were of how good it would feel to kill the fucker with his bare hands, although he knew that might not be too helpful at this point.

Aiden snickered as Frank pulled up in the main street of Almondine. This was going to be fun.

"We'll try the sheriff's office first," Frank announced, putting on his hat. He was always well-dressed, and today was no exception. His brown boots shone and his corduroy pants were well-fitted. His plain cream shirt was neatly tucked into his waistband and his belt buckle gleamed in the afternoon sun. He walked with the confident gait of an older man as they crossed the street and strolled up the steps to the open doorway.

"I'm really hoping you can help me, Deputy Taylor," a familiar woman's voice said from inside. "Robert told me you're the best, so I'm kind of relying on you."

"I'll do everything I can, Miss Parry." Cam Taylor sounded gruff and a little unnerved.

Frank reared, almost knocking Aiden back down the steps. He put a finger to his mouth in a gesture of silence then stood with his back to the wall just by the doorway.

Aiden frowned but followed suit.

"I know you will. And, of course, there'll be a reward for the return of my necklace. You see, it had great sentimental value to me, but obviously Robert doesn't know that." She lowered her voice conspiratorially. "Perhaps we could keep this between us?"

"Yeah, sure..." Cam Taylor seemed to have perked up all of a sudden. "I'll do my best to get it returned to you. You just leave everything to me — and, of course, mum's the word."

Aiden grimaced, wondering just how naïve Lorraine was. Maybe it was time to find out.

He pointed to the ground, indicating to Frank that he was planning to stay put. Frank nodded and slowly strolled into the office.

Aiden peeped around the door and saw Frank stand with his back to Lorraine, carefully studying a large notice board at one side of the room.

"Well, I can see I'm in safe hands," Lorraine remarked as her heels clicked across the wooden floor.

Aiden quickly made his way down the steps and leaned nonchalantly across the rail at the bottom as the blonde-haired woman came out. He watched her give a tiny smirk as she stood on the top step, then carefully but confidently walked down the steps toward him.

"Hi, Lorraine." He smiled as he raised his hat to her.

"Aiden, how nice to see you again." She beamed at him, blushing slightly. "What brings you out here?"

"Frank's got some business to attend to in town," Aiden told her, shrugging. "I thought I'd tag along for the ride, but I didn't want to get involved. How about you?"

"I had some jewelry stolen recently. Deputy Taylor's promised to look into it for me."

Aiden frowned, surprised that she didn't look more concerned about her loss. "That's awful. Do they know who did it?"

She chewed her lip hesitantly. "You got time for a coffee?"

"Sure thing." Aiden jumped at the chance.

Lorraine linked his arm then led him up the street to the nearby diner where they took a table in a quiet corner.

Aiden ordered their coffees, aware of the way Lorraine studied his face. He turned to smile at her, wondering what she was thinking just then.

"You're very like your brother, aren't you?" she answered his unasked question with one of her own.

"No, I like to think I got the brains as *well* as looks," he said with a grin.

She hooted. "I'll tell Ben you said that," she teased, just as the waitress put their drinks on the table.

"I think he likes you," Aiden noted.

Lorraine flushed and immediately busied herself adding cream to her coffee. "I like him, too," she confided.

Aiden smiled. He could certainly see why his brother was attracted to her. Lorraine was quite pretty when she smiled, although not as attractive as Maggie, in his mind.

"We got to talking," she went on in a hushed tone. "Ben told me about that misunderstanding with Maggie. I hope I didn't make things worse?"

Aiden sipped his coffee, then asked, "In what way?"

"Just by being there, I guess. It must have been awful for her, especially with Robert's reaction. He can be very... *insensitive* at times."

Aiden raised his eyebrows. Perhaps she wasn't as taken in by Robert Rossington as he had feared.

She smiled. "It's all right. Robert stole the necklace from me. It wasn't worth quite as much as he took from Maggie, but it was still unforgiveable."

Aiden stared at her. "You *know*?"

She took a sip of her drink, eyeing him thoughtfully. "Robert stole all Maggie's money and got Cam Taylor to fabricate some story about being robbed." She nodded slowly. "And now he's stolen my necklace and is paying Deputy Taylor to cover that up, too."

Aiden frowned. "Is that why you were in the sheriff's office today?"

She nodded. "I've told the guy that there will be a large reward if he can get my necklace back. He seemed real interested, too."

Aiden narrowed his eyes. "So you think Taylor's got it?"

She shook her head, picking up her cup. "No. Robert's still got it," she told him matter-of-factly. "It'll be interesting to see how Cam Taylor gets it off him, but I reckon he will."

"So he can claim your reward?"

She nodded. "My guess is he won't mention that part to Robert. He'll just get it off him and return it to me. Taylor thinks I'm offering the reward because the necklace is of great sentimental value to me, something I won't have admitted to Robert."

Aiden took a slow sip of his coffee, eyeing her curiously. "And you're sure it was Robert who took it?"

She nodded, a little sadly. "Yeah, he took it all right. He obviously didn't notice the CCTV in my dressing room. I've got the tape under lock and key."

"Unlike the necklace?" Aiden snickered.

Lorraine laughed. "Not exactly, though he did have to hunt for it," she explained. "Well, it wouldn't have been any fun if it had been too easy, would it?"

Aiden chortled. "I like the way you think," he said.

"Funnily enough, your brother does too," she confided with a salacious smile that made him laugh even more.

"I can see why Ben likes you," he said, giving her an impressed nod. "You're both pretty outrageous."

"I can't deny that," she responded, taking another sip of her drink.

"So how come Robert's not around?" Aiden looked around the diner, half-expecting her fiancé to suddenly turn up.

"Don't worry about him. He's out of town today. And I can guess where he'll be tonight too, once Taylor calls him."

"You reckon they'll meet up tonight?" He frowned.

"Oh yeah." She smiled confidently. "Taylor will want to get his hands on that necklace as soon as he can. I wouldn't be surprised if he hasn't called him already. Robert's over in Springvale today, seeing who'll offer him the best price for it."

Aiden gaped. "How on earth did you find that out?"

She smirked. "You really were taken in by my 'dumb blonde' act the other night, weren't you? Well, let me tell you..." She lowered her voice conspiratorially. "Not only am I not so dumb, but I'm not a natural blonde, either." She giggled.

Aiden just stared at her.

"I had a boyfriend, Chuck, before I moved away," she explained, taking another sip of her coffee. "I was totally besotted with him, but my daddy saw right through him. The guy started stealing my cash, and, when he couldn't get that, he used to take whatever he could from the house. Daddy was doing some business over at Springvale when he saw a couple of Momma's silver vases in a pawn shop over there. Didn't take long to discover my beloved boyfriend had been making quite a bit of money selling our stuff that way. Luckily, Daddy had connections, so he was able to pull in a few favors." She chewed her lip.

"That must have been awful for you," Aiden replied softly, seeing the clouded look on her face.

She grimaced. "I didn't believe it. Well... I didn't *want* to believe it. I told Daddy he must have gotten it wrong. That's when he took me over there to see for myself. It's a strange feeling seeing something you just assumed was still back at home sitting there on the shelf of some musty, old second-hand shop. Daddy introduced me to the owners, and they each gave the same description of the guy who'd brought the stuff in to them. It was Chuck all right. Hadn't even had the sense to cover the tattoo on his arm."

"Ouch!" Aiden winced at the thought of finding all that out the hard way.

She smirked. "It was then I realized what a grade-A jerk the guy was. I vowed I'd never fall for a dipshit like that again. Then I met Robert."

Aiden really felt for the woman. She'd sure had her share of asshats.

She shook her head. "I was a bit savvier this time," she told him. "I thought he was quite sweet when we first got together, but I could read the signs all right. I always seemed to be the one to pay when we went out, and he used to make up all sorts of excuses not to take me back to his place. He still doesn't think I know where he lives." She shrugged.

"So you're not actually planning to marry him then?" Aiden felt a sense of relief.

She shook her head. "Of course not. He's only after my money. I know that."

Aiden narrowed his eyes. "So you're planning to expose him?"

"I wasn't going to at first. I thought I'd just stop seeing him and that would be that. But then he got drunk one night and bragged to some guy about how he'd swindled Maggie out of her money. I only found out by accident while I was checking some tapes. I'd had some cameras installed around the house when Mom started needing home help. I just wanted to make sure they were looking after her properly while I wasn't there, you know? Anyhow, at first I was horrified that he'd do a thing like that, then I realized if he could do it once, he could do it again. It was like a red rag to a bull. I was so mad that I decided then and there I was going to make dang sure he didn't get to do it to any other poor woman. I'll see him go down for this. You see if I don't."

Aiden saw her jaw tense as she filled him in on a few more details, and he knew this girl meant business. He'd seen that look before on Maggie's face not so long ago.

"Good for you," he told her.

She finished her coffee. "Hey, we should let Maggie know we're on to him." Her eyes lit up.

Aiden felt his heart lift, and he grinned. "Well if Robert's out of town, there's nothing stopping us going over there right now, is there?" He was desperate to see Maggie again, to make sure she was all right.

"Going where?" Frank suddenly appeared, smiling.

"We thought we'd go over and tell Maggie about Lorraine's plan to smoke out Rossington," he murmured. "The guy won't be around for a couple of hours, so it's a golden opportunity, and it'll make Maggie's day to know there's a plan in place."

Frank's face lit up. "I had an idea you were hatching something," he said to Lorraine with a surreptitious smile.

"Now I remember you. I thought I recognized you in the sheriff's office, but I wasn't sure." Lorraine pointed at Frank as she spoke.

"Did you unearth anything?" Aiden asked as Frank took the seat next to him.

The old man gave a satisfied nod. "Oh yeah. He's on the take, all right. I told him I was moving into one of those big old houses down by the river and just wanted to know about security and stuff. He offered to keep a 'special eye' on the place for a small monthly fee." He used air quotes to emphasize his meaning.

"Yeah, I can imagine his idea of 'small', too." Aiden also used air quotes, and they all giggled at the implications.

"Well, I'd best get back to Sylvia," Frank said. "You need a ride back?" He looked questioningly at them.

"I'm heading over to see Maggie now, if you wanna come?" Lorraine offered.

Aiden nodded. "That'd be great."

* * * *

Maggie was just wiping down the last of the tables when the door swung open and Aiden walked in. She couldn't hide the massive beam which spread across her face.

"What're you doing here? I thought—" She gasped.

Aiden was dressed in a white shirt that was tight enough to show off his muscles and jeans tight enough to show something else!

Ignoring the last couple of customers, he scooped her into his arms, and she felt his hot body flush against hers as he took her lips in a sensual kiss that left her tingling for more.

"He's out of town," he whispered into her ear once he'd unlocked their mouths. "And I've got news."

Her heart was pounding with hope as she gazed into his gorgeous face. He was obviously dying to tell her something and looked like he was going to burst if he didn't let it out soon.

He managed to wait until the customers finally left and they were alone. Maggie momentarily wondered if they wouldn't complain to her boss about her kissing in the café, but somehow she didn't care about that right now.

She was about to go and lock the door but noticed a large car outside that she didn't recognize.

"Aiden, are you *sure* the coast is clear?" She frowned, her heart now pounding for a totally different reason. She could hear someone talking outside and couldn't be certain that Robert hadn't sent someone to spy on them. "I know you hate having to stay apart as much as I do, and I'm sure Robert wouldn't hurt me if you were with me, but…"

"But we won't be able to nail the guy if he knows we're together." He nodded, though he didn't seem very worried. "Then we wouldn't be able to get him to return all the money he took from you."

She shook her head, realizing for the umpteenth time how ludicrous it all sounded. "You really think we've got a chance of getting my money back? I mean, it's been a couple of years, and I'm still no closer to proving anything. The longer it goes on, the worse my chances get. I'll never be able to prove he did it. I really don't know why you think you can just—" She broke off as someone walked in the door.

"Aiden may not be able to prove he stole your cash, Maggie," the woman told her as she slowly strolled toward the counter, "but *I* can."

Chapter Thirteen

Lorraine Parry gave a mischievous smile as she took a stool at the counter.

"Coffee?" Maggie eyed her curiously, already pouring her drink.

Lorraine nodded as Maggie placed the coffee in front of her. She stared at Maggie's bruise and winced, horrified. "Robert did that?"

Maggie nodded. "It's not the first time," she shared.

Lorraine bit her beautifully painted lip. "I thought he was gonna hit me the other day," she confided. "I had no idea he was capable of anything like that, though."

"He's capable of a lot more, believe me," Maggie replied.

Lorraine swallowed hard.

"Is it a good idea for you to be seen with me?" Maggie suddenly realized that Lorraine might be putting herself in danger by being here.

"It's okay. He's over at Springvale. I've just had confirmation from his hotel that he's arrived and found the bar, so he won't be bothering anyone for a while."

"Sounds about right." Maggie nodded.

"She knows he stole your money," Aiden explained to Maggie as he locked the door and pulled the blind down.

Maggie frowned.

"It didn't take Miss Marple," Lorraine told them, raising her eyebrows. "You know what Robert's like with a few drinks in him. He was singing like a canary — boasting, actually." She sniggered. "Luckily, I'd had the house wired up with cameras as soon as I realized I'd have to hire help to look after Mom. You hear such awful things these days.

I couldn't risk anything happening to her."

"Is she okay?" Maggie asked softly.

"She's got dementia. I didn't know until I got back for Daddy's funeral. I've got her the best help, though, and they really are looking after her." Lorraine nodded.

"So you've actually recorded Rossington admitting to stealing Maggie's cash?" Aiden smirked.

"Oh yeah. I've got the tape with the proof, but that's just part of it." Lorraine grinned conspiratorially. "I knew he'd still try to lie his way out of it," Lorraine continued as they all sat around the counter. "So I had a good nosey around his computer and found some rather interesting emails that took place between Robert and Cam Taylor over at Almondine."

Maggie frowned. "That's the guy from the sheriff's office. He was supposed to have investigated the theft of my money."

"That's him." Lorraine nodded. "Seems he and Robert were as thick as…well, *thieves*."

"So you can prove they stole my money?" Maggie felt hope well in her for the first time in ages. "Have you been to the sheriff?"

Lorraine sighed. "I spoke to Dyson Shearer about it, but he thinks it could be construed as circumstantial. There's conversations about them both meeting up and dates when you'd be out of town, but the sheriff said that with a good lawyer, Robert could still get around it."

"Then there's no hope." Maggie put her elbows on the counter and covered her face with her hands. "I should have known."

"Not necessarily." Lorraine smirked. "I've also got proof that Robert stole from *me*. It's all on camera. And guess who's investigating that theft?"

Maggie moved her hands from her face and stared at Lorraine incredulously. "Not Cam Taylor?"

"The very same," Lorraine told her with a giggle. "And now that Deputy Taylor knows that I'd be *so* grateful for the return of my jewelry — and the size of the reward involved — I'd be very surprised if it doesn't somehow materialize real soon."

"So, with all that, as well as the evidence about my money, they've got to accept it's the truth." Maggie felt ready to explode with relief.

"I'd best get back to my mom," Lorraine said. "You take care, Maggie."

"I will, and thanks for stopping by." Maggie couldn't resist going over and giving her a hug. Although Lorraine Parry was stick-thin, she sure gave good hugs, and Maggie relished her warmth.

Maggie quickly stacked the washer and wiped down the counter while Aiden saw Lorraine out. She was already putting her coat on when he came back inside.

"Lorraine offered us a ride as I haven't brought my car, but I said we'd enjoy a stroll home. Is that okay with you?" he asked as he slung an arm around her and led her to the door. "I thought we could pick up a carry-out on the way?"

His words were music to her ears. "Home as in *my* home?" She tried to keep the tremble of excitement from her voice. "You want to come back to my place?"

He chuckled as they began to walk. "If that's all right with you? I mean, we could grab a cab and go back to mine if you'd prefer?"

"No, no, it's fine," she assured him.

She was thrilled that he had referred to her tiny apartment as 'home'. The last time he had been there, she had been convinced that he would be horrified with where she lived, and after throwing him out, she really didn't think he'd want to return.

"As that bastard's out for the night, I thought we may as well make hay while the sun shines — or, rather, the moon, in our case." He was smiling wickedly down at her.

She smiled. "I like that idea."

Not only did they fetch a Chinese carry-out, but they also popped into the supermarket for a large tub of Ben and

Jerry's.

"I fancy dessert tonight," he said, giving her a salacious wink.

Maggie felt her face flush as her heart beat a little faster.

She quickly locked the door behind them once they got back to her apartment. She turned around to see he had already put the food down before swooping her into his warm arms. She had missed him more than she'd realized, and Maggie clung onto him tightly as his heady scent surrounded her.

"How long's Robert out of town for?" she asked, hopefully, when he finally freed her mouth.

"Just tonight, Lorraine reckons. We think he's gone to meet up with Cam Taylor."

Maggie felt a jolt in her stomach. "Why?"

Aiden sighed, leading her into the kitchen where he snagged a couple of forks and spoons from a china utensil jar on the counter. "Lorraine told you how she went to see Taylor today to tell him she was prepared to give a hefty reward for the safe return of her necklace?"

Maggie nodded as she curled up next to him on the old sofa and tucked into her chicken chow mein.

"She reckons Rossington's still got it. He was probably planning to get rid of it today. It's worth quite a bit. Trouble is, now Taylor wants it, so it's a whole new ball game."

Maggie popped some chicken into her mouth, then moaned.

Aiden chuckled.

"Do you think Robert will give it to him?" she asked thoughtfully.

"Maybe. For a price."

"But they could claim the reward if Taylor gives it back to Lorraine. Surely that's a win-win?"

Aiden shook his head as he ate his meal. "Not gonna happen. Rossington doesn't know about the reward. When Taylor returns the necklace to Lorraine, he'll claim it for himself."

Maggie thought for a while as they ate. "But won't Robert know when Lorraine hands over the money?" she asked at last.

"She won't tell him, and Taylor knows it. As far as Cam Taylor knows, the necklace was bought for her by someone special — a fact that Rossington doesn't realize. She couldn't explain away her need to get it back without admitting that it's got sentimental value. And don't forget, Rossington thinks they're going to marry. He won't be too pleased with the thought of her hanging on to something from some ex-lover."

Maggie gasped. Lorraine really seemed to have this all worked out. Maggie stacked up the empty plates then snuggled back into Aiden's side when he opened the Ben and Jerry's.

"There's no honor among thieves," Aiden pointed out, feeding her a scoop of ice cream.

"So what will happen?" Maggie frowned, staring up at him.

"I wouldn't be surprised if it led to a fight."

Despite the ice cream, she felt herself go hot.

"If Lorraine's got proof that Robert took her jewelry, why doesn't she just show Dyson the tape? He can't deny it if it's right there in front of him, surely?" Maggie waved her spoon around as she figured it all out.

"But all that will prove is that Rossington took the necklace. It won't help get your money back, and, with a good lawyer, he'll be able to get a lighter sentence. I dunno, claim forgetfulness or a moment of madness or whatever. You know how these things work. And besides, Cam Taylor will get off scot-free." Aiden teased her with another spoonful of ice cream. He put the spoon to her lips, then pulled it away a couple of times, making her giggle, before she finally grabbed his hand and devoured the dessert. After savoring the taste, she thought for a moment.

"I don't really understand why she wants to help get my money back, anyhow," Maggie admitted. "I mean, it's real nice of her and all, but I don't get why she's bothering."

Aiden snickered. "She's a woman scorned," he said to her. "She told me all about it. Her last boyfriend stole from her, and she was danged if it was going to happen again. Seems she was taken in by Rossington at first, though it didn't last long. When she realized what his game was, the same as her previous guy, she was furious—not to mention hurt. No one likes to be made to look a fool, and that's exactly what the fucker had done to her and what Rossington was planning to do. The same as he'd done to you." He kissed her lightly on the forehead. "She was checking one of those tapes to see that her mother had been looked after properly while she'd been out, when she caught Rossington boasting about how he'd swindled you out of your money. He'd gone off into the front room with some of the guys after dinner, obviously not realizing she'd had the house wired. He'd also made some comment on there about how stupid *she* was. Her first instinct was to confront him, but then she decided to play the long game—expose him for the thieving bastard he is. That's when she started digging."

Maggie chewed her cheek. "So why bother with the necklace?"

Aiden popped the last spoonful of ice cream into her mouth. "I think she just wanted proof that he would actually steal from *her*, as well as you. When Rossington insisted on going to Taylor to investigate it instead of calling Dyson Shearer, she went along with it."

"So now she's going to pit them against each other." The thought, coupled with the amount of ice cream she had just consumed, made Maggie feel sick.

"I don't think that was her intention, but it sure will be interesting." Aiden raised his eyebrows as he leaned forward and put the empty tub on the coffee table in front of them. "You don't have to worry."

"He'll be mad as hell. You don't know what he's capable of," she said, shaking her head.

"Why don't you just relax? At least he's finally given us

the chance to spend some time together." Aiden smiled sensually as he leaned in and took her lips in a lingering kiss that sent shivers down her back.

Maggie sighed when he put his arms around her, and she snuggled in closer as his kiss deepened.

He teased the seam of her lips with his soft tongue until she opened her mouth to welcome him in and she threaded her fingers in his hair, moaning when she felt herself getting warmer when his hot body pressed tightly to hers.

Something about his reassuring manner and confident moves soothed her, and her stress eased while his competent hands roamed her body. She gasped as he explored her mouth with his tongue before sucking at her neck and nibbling her ears, sending delicious shivers through her whole body.

For the first time in years, Maggie felt her pussy ache when the handsome cowboy leaned over her panting body, sending new sensations through her, awakening feelings she thought were long dead.

His frame was hard against her softness, and she relished the feel of his muscles as he held her assuredly. After carefully leaning her back on the sofa, he lay over her, surrounding her with his warmth, his scent. Aiden traced her cheek with his finger and she pressed her face into his hand, staring into his deep, blue eyes that gazed back at her dreamily.

Her nipples had tightened, and she was sure he could feel how large and proud they had become. Her pussy throbbed, and she was surprised to find herself willing him to touch it.

Aiden raised his eyebrow questioningly, and she wondered if he could read her mind. The smile on his face suggested that he knew exactly what she was thinking, and the thought made her flush.

"You okay?" he murmured, taking her hand and kissing her fingertips.

When she didn't reply, he nipped the top of her middle

finger, and she jolted in surprise. His questioning gaze returned to her face, and she nodded.

He threw her a dazzling smile and chuckled deep in his chest, sending delectable vibrations through her trembling body.

A cold shudder ran down her when he slowly eased his weight from her, studying her face intently.

"It's a little warmer in the bedroom," she murmured, noticing his concern.

He beamed and let out a low chuckle while he lifted himself off her. He put out his hand to help her up and she took it, relishing its warmth.

Butterflies danced a two-step in her stomach as she led him into her little room. The drapes were still back, allowing a sliver of moonlight to cast a welcoming glow on her bed. The carpet wasn't quite as threadbare here as in the major parts of the apartment, and she had put a fluffy rug right next to the bed, adding another layer of heat and a soft, coziness underfoot.

Aiden didn't seem to notice her décor, however. His gaze was fixed on her face. Slowly he pushed her back onto the firm bed, watching her expression.

Maggie felt hot and excited when she toed off her boots and kicked them onto the floor. He kicked his off, too, still not taking his eyes from her. His intense stare unnerved her a little, and she took a deep breath to try to steady her thoughts.

"You sure you're up to this?" His voice was low and soft, while his eyes were wide and cautious.

At first she felt confused, then she remembered her face was still covered in bruises. She was touched that he was considerate enough to ask the question, but she really hoped that her injuries wouldn't put him off.

"I'm fine, honestly." She smiled, desperate to reassure him.

It seemed to work as he beamed back at her, gently laying his body over her. His lips encased hers once again, and she sighed into his mouth. His affection soothed her once more. She was glad that she had dispensed with her sweater earlier. His nimble fingers made short work of her buttons before slowly opening her blouse, exposing her. Maggie watched his eyes widen even more and his lips turned up into a broad smile when he gazed down at her heaving bosom. She had never seen anyone react so favorably to her body before, and she immediately relaxed.

"You are so beautiful, Maggie," he whispered.

She felt herself flush and she gazed into his gorgeous face. Everything about him was sincere, and she felt empowered by his approval. Very deliberately he began to unfasten his own shirt, until her hands covered his and she took over from him. He grinned down at her patiently as her trembling fingers fumbled a little with his buttons, but she soon managed to peel the cotton from his heated body, and he pulled his arms through the sleeves, flinging the garment onto the rug.

Maggie drew in a sharp breath at the sight of his ripped chest. Without his clothes, Aiden looked even bigger somehow, and she loved the way his deep, steady breaths made his torso swell even more. A few fair hairs were scattered over his rib cage and his six-pack was a delight. His muscular shoulders bulged. Aiden caressed her breasts through the lace, and she glanced down to see her dark nipples standing to attention beneath his hands. He pulled down the fabric from her left breast and lavished affection on her swollen nipple before he took it into his mouth.

Maggie groaned at the sensation and had to clench her pussy hard as her juices began to escape.

He continued his delicious torment on the other breast, and she felt a moment's trepidation when his hand came around her back and unfastened her bra, leaving her heavy breasts to bounce free. Aiden's eyes were like two large lagoons as they took in the sight of her body, and she smiled, relieved at his approval. She had always felt that her body was too large in all aspects, and Robert had done nothing to

110

quell her fears. Aiden made her feel beautiful, though, and he couldn't hide his enjoyment at looking at her.

Aiden ground his body on hers while he licked and sucked at her soft breasts, and she relished the feel of his skin touching her. His erection was apparent through his denims, and she gasped when his massive cock rubbed against her throbbing pussy.

As if reading her thoughts, he trailed his hand down to her zipper and carefully tugged at the metal pull. Maggie went red hot with excitement as he sat back on his haunches and his capable fingers slid the jeans from her legs. His look of delight gave her even more confidence, and she reached over for his fly. He chuckled, leaning closer so she could easily pull the zipper down, and he worked the thick material down his legs.

Maggie gasped, noticing that he went commando, and she balked at the monstrous size of his manhood as it sprang to attention as soon as it was free.

A gush of juice escaped her, reminding her that she was just lying there staring at the guy's cock. She flushed and quickly looked away, hoping he hadn't noticed. His chuckle told her that he had noticed all right. *Damn!*

His eyes twinkled while he lay over her once more, and she smiled. It was great to be with a guy who had a sense of humor as well as the sensitivity she needed.

He danced his fingers across her stomach and she felt it dip as she gasped. His touch was so light that it tickled her, sending delightful shivers through her body.

"I think these will have to go." His hand drifted down to the waistband of her panties that were plastered to her skin because they had become so wet.

She was relieved when he'd removed them and glad that they hadn't switched on the light. The moonlight was enough for her to make out Aiden's silhouette and to see his expression when he lay back over her, but it was not bright enough to make her feel entirely exposed.

He crashed his mouth down on hers again as he covered

her naked body with his own. His scent mingled with sweat and passion while he surrounded her in his affection.

Maggie stroked his firm flesh, loving the feel of skin on skin as he rubbed against her, lighting sparks through her over-sensitized form.

"I want you, Maggie." His voice was rasping — desperate, almost — when he stared down at her.

She felt her pussy gush once more and knew there was no going back. She wanted this, needed it. Needed *him*.

"Yes," she gasped, unable to say much else.

He reached beside her and grabbed a foil packet that he must have dropped there when he'd removed his jeans, and he quickly tore it between his teeth. His eyes never left hers as he sheathed himself and tenderly fondled her dripping folds before plunging into her depths.

Maggie let out a cry when his enormous manhood filled her to the hilt. Concern was etched in his face as he stopped to take a breath, but he needn't have worried. Once her body adjusted around his massive girth, she clenched him tightly, trying to suck him even tighter into her body. She never wanted him to leave. This was where she wanted him to be, forever. Wrapping her legs around his butt, she pulled him even closer, wanting to get underneath his skin. The feelings he bestowed on her were out of this world, and she knew she could never feel like this with anyone else.

As though reading her mind, Aiden continued to bombard her with delectable sensations while he hammered harder and harder into her. Sweat poured from him, and his breath was ragged. He drove deeper and deeper into her willing body.

Maggie found it hard to catch her breath as she was swamped with feelings she had never imagined. It was as though Aiden's body knew every inch of hers — knew how to tease, how to coax, how to take her to the edge and —

"Aah!" She screamed into the darkness when her orgasm exploded around her and she screwed her eyes tight. Tiny stars burst all around her head.

Aiden roared his release, and she started at how feral he sounded, nothing like the gentle, considerate lover he was.

Finally spent, he sank onto the bed next to her, allowing the air to waft over her heated body. Her eyes closed as she turned to lay her head gently on his chest, needing his nearness, but favoring her space while she slowly descended back to Earth.

Maggie listened to the pounding of his heart while the heaving of his chest gradually eased and his breathing returned to normal. She loved the smell of him, the salty taste of his skin and the sound of his voice when he murmured to her how lovely she was and how wonderful it had been to make love to her. She had never felt more content in her life — or more wanted.

Chapter Fourteen

Maggie woke with a huge smile spread across her face the next morning, and, judging by the way her muscles ached, she guessed she had been that way most of the night. Instead of the dark, scary dreams she usually endured, she had been dreaming of love and sunny days and happily-ever-afters for the first time in a very long time.

She looked over at Aiden, who was sleeping soundly next to her. He was smiling and looked contented, too. She couldn't help wondering what he was dreaming about, and she hoped it involved her. A warm glow emanated from her stomach, and she wondered what it would be like to wake up next to him every morning.

His eyes fluttered open, and his smile broadened. "Morning, darlin'." He sounded chirpy straight-off, and his arm tightened a little around her shoulder.

"Good morning." She beamed at him and felt his warmth as he leaned down and kissed her tenderly.

Immediately her pussy tensed, and she knew she wanted him all over again. Her stomach started to burn as the fire ignited inside her, and she flushed.

A deep chuckle reverberated through his body, tickling her breast that was now pressed hard against his chest. She knew he'd read her mind. She also knew it was only Wednesday, and they both had work to do. *Damn!*

Slowly pulling away from him, she turned to check the time. "Oh my God! Aiden, it's half past seven!" She startled then leaped out of the bed.

"I'll get the coffee on," he offered as she fled toward the bathroom.

The water felt good on her tender flesh, and she smiled as she remembered how her body had become so achy. She had never had a night like it. Aiden was the most caring, intuitive lover she had ever had – not that she'd had many – and she knew she would never want anyone else. It wasn't just the way he made her feel in bed. It was... something more – the way he made her feel all the time. He made her happy. Even when she had been mad at him, she had known she really still wanted to see him again.

After wrapping herself in a towel, she scrubbed her teeth before pulling a comb through her wayward curls.

"Is it my turn yet?"

She spun around and opened the door to see Aiden leaning against the doorjamb wearing nothing but a small towel and a huge smile. He was offering her a cup of steaming coffee, and she drank in the whole sight of him. She smiled, taking the mug from his hand.

"I almost jumped in there with you, but I figured we'd never get to work today if I did," he murmured, giving her a salacious wink.

She grinned. He was absolutely right. If she had her way, they would both spend the day making love and probably wouldn't even stop to eat. "Work? What's work?" She smiled cheekily before taking a sip. He sure made great coffee. "Hey, this is really good. Maybe you should get a job in the café."

He chuckled. "If you don't get moving, you won't have a job down there yourself." He playfully swatted her behind through her towel as he stood back to allow her to go into the bedroom.

She felt a sudden pang inside her as reality returned with a vengeance. "You're right," she said, sighing.

"Hey, don't sweat it, darlin'. You won't be there much longer anyhow," he told her with a knowing smile.

"I hope you're right."

"Trust me." He leaned over and kissed her wet head.

Maggie felt that warmth return again. She did trust him.

She knew he would do whatever he could to help her. He cared about her more than anyone ever had in her whole life. Something just felt right about being with Aiden.

"I'll be out in minute," he said. "Why don't you call a cab? It'll save some time."

She was just about to reply that she never called a cab because she couldn't afford one, but she knew by the look on his face that it wasn't what he wanted to hear. She smiled and went to find her clothes.

The bruise on her face was beginning to fade at last, so it didn't take too long for her apply her makeup and dry her hair.

Aiden was ready in a jiffy. It was amazing how little effort it took him to look so good. Even in yesterday's clothes and using a borrowed comb, he looked gorgeous.

They rushed out when they heard the cab beeping, and they piled into the back seat. Aiden automatically held his arm out to her, and Maggie snuggled into his warm body. It was good to feel close again after the mad rush they'd had to get ready.

"I'll come in for another coffee," he said when the cab pulled up outside the café a few minutes later.

Maggie smiled. She didn't want him to leave her. Aiden seemed to make everything right. And now everything *was* right. While she went through her normal routine of opening up the café and getting the coffee and bread on, she felt relaxed and happy. Soon Robert would be out of their hair, and, with any luck, she would at least have a chance of getting her money back. She could move out of that awful apartment and leave this job for good. She gazed over at Aiden, who had plunked himself on his usual seat by the counter. She wondered what she would do when she didn't have to come here anymore, and she found herself hoping wistfully that whatever it was, it would involve the handsome cowboy.

"I won't stay long," he whispered to her when her first customers arrived for breakfast.

She felt a sudden pang but quickly admonished herself for her selfishness. Of course she was going to miss him, but Aiden had a ranch to run, and she had to keep her mind on her job—at least for now.

As she smiled back at him, she noticed he was looking warily out of the window, and she suddenly remembered that Robert might be back at any time. It wouldn't look good if he found them together, and it could stir up a whole load more trouble for them all.

"Looks like I'm gonna be kept busy," she said, nodding to a crowd of cowboys who had just piled in through the door.

Aiden grinned, taking his hat from the seat next to him. "In that case, I'd best leave you to it," he responded, before leaning over to give her a chaste kiss on the cheek.

Maggie flushed, thrilled that he didn't mind showing his emotions in front of her customers. She smiled as he swaggered toward the door, and her heart leapt when he stopped to give her a salacious wink just before he left.

* * * *

Aiden took a good look around the area outside the café while he waited for a cab to pick him up. He wanted to make dang sure that Rossington wasn't spying on Maggie. He had to make sure his girl was safe before he left her.

"*My* girl," he mused as he jumped into the cab. He was surprised how possessive he felt about the gorgeous waitress. His thoughts wandered back to last night and a huge smile spread across his face. He felt like he had done nothing but smile since he'd woken up this morning. Last night had sure been something else. The journey home was a blur, as he couldn't concentrate on anything except Maggie. He was determined to show her just how much she meant to him. It had been lovely to see her looking so relaxed today, and he wanted her to always look like that. In order to achieve that, though, he would first have to sort out this whole mess with Rossington.

He quickly refreshed himself then changed once he got home, before going to find his brother. Ben was out by the training paddock talking to Frank Crowthorne.

"No prizes for guessing where you got to," Ben remarked as Aiden joined them.

"My lips are sealed," he replied.

"Yeah, and they're also beaming from ear to ear," Ben replied with a chuckle. "Your expression speaks volumes, bro."

Aiden felt himself smile even more. He was glad they could see how happy Maggie made him. He was proud to be seeing such a beautiful girl.

"I've got some news," Frank said. "I've heard from an old colleague of mine, Alex Carrass, over at the attorney's office."

Aiden felt his face fall a little.

"Seems Rossington's been over there asking about possible loopholes in the conditions Jake Parry set in his will." Frank smirked, which Aiden immediately found reassuring.

"And?" He hardly dared ask.

Frank shook his head. "It's watertight. Parry knew what he was doing, all right. Looks like he hired the best to make sure the ranch was protected. That land can't leave the family. The only way Rossington can get anywhere near it is to join the Parrys."

"And there ain't no way Lorraine's gonna let him do that." Ben sounded quite sure of the fact.

Aiden narrowed his eyes. "Did they tell Rossington this?" He looked warily at Frank.

"Not yet. He's got an appointment over there around lunchtime today."

Aiden felt a lurch in his stomach. "He'll be hopping mad this afternoon, then."

Ben shrugged. "There ain't nothin' he can do about it. The law's the law. Right, Frank?" He looked over at the older man.

Frank nodded. "Yeah, but Aiden's right. Once Rossington hears his plan's doomed, he'll be like a bear with a bee sting. We'd better keep an eye on the girls."

"No problem. I'll get on over to Lorraine's as soon as I get done with the veterinarian." Ben put on his hat, about to leave.

"What if Rossington goes over there? He's not gonna be too happy to see you with his fiancée?" Aiden frowned.

"Don't you worry about that. I've promised to do a few jobs about the place to make life easier for Martha. As far as Rossington knows, I'm just a neighbor doing them a favor." Ben obviously had it all worked out.

Aiden shook his head as his brother made his way toward his truck.

"I'll be in the stables if you need me," Ben called over.

Aiden nodded.

"What about Maggie? You can't be seen over there," Frank warned him.

Aiden sighed. "I can't just leave her on her own. What if he takes it out on her? He's already hit her." He felt his blood boil at the thought. He should have been there for her that night. He should never have let her...

"We'll figure something out," Frank assured him. "Even if I happen to pop over for a coffee, it won't look too suspicious."

Aiden felt a surge of relief. Frank was right. Rossington was unlikely to recognize him from the party, anyhow. He had been so drunk that it would be a miracle if he recalled anything about that night.

"Thanks, Frank."

The older man smiled. "I'll look out for her. Don't you worry, son."

Aiden grinned. He knew he wore his heart on his sleeve and didn't mind one bit that the people around him could see how much he cared for the blonde beauty. As long as Rossington didn't get wind of it, he wasn't bothered who knew.

* * * *

Maggie was pleasantly surprised when Frank sauntered into the café later that afternoon. She smiled at him, remembering that she was supposed to act as though she didn't know him. Not that she suspected any of the customers as having anything to do with Robert, but it was good to keep on the safe side.

"I'll take coffee and a cinnamon donut please, miss." He sat by the window with a clear view to the door.

She placed his order in front of him just as his cell rang. Frank frowned as he took the call, and Maggie left him to his privacy.

There weren't many other customers in the café, so she busied herself with cleaning down the counters and generally puttering about. She couldn't hear what Frank was saying on the phone, but he sure seemed engrossed in his conversation. It was nice to see him here, and she felt a little more secure having him around.

By the time Frank had finished his coffee, most of the customers had left. There was just one elderly couple remaining in one of the booths at the far end of the restaurant when he hailed for a top-up of his drink.

"Everything okay?" she murmured as she poured it out.

"I'm not sure," Frank confided in a hushed tone. "Ben's over at the Parry's right now. He's doing some odd jobs for Martha, who told him that she remembered Rossington being around there. Seems Jake was doing some deal with him, but she didn't know the details. That's how he and Lorraine met."

Maggie frowned. "This is the old lady with dementia?"

Frank nodded. "That's right. Don't underestimate her, though, Maggie. Martha Parry has dementia, but she's not stupid. If she says Rossington was in her house, I believe her."

Maggie nodded. "I'm right with you, Frank. I had an uncle with dementia and, although some days he didn't remember his own name, other times he was as sharp as a tack."

"Awful business." Frank shook his head knowingly. "Anyhow, Ben's going to check with Lorraine if there was anything in the company documents about any dealings between them. Jake was a stickler for the paperwork. If there was something going, he would have gotten it in writing."

Maggie wiped his table before going to check on her other customers. The elderly couple were about to leave, and they left her a generous tip, for which she was sincerely thankful.

She was hoping for a chance to chat with Frank some more, but as they closed the door, it immediately opened again and a crowd of rowdy youngsters flooded in. She noticed Frank taking another call as she poured their drinks and couldn't help wishing she could hear what he was saying. After that, it became busy again for a while before petering off just before closing time.

"I'll give you a ride home," he announced when everyone else had left at last.

She frowned. "It's real nice of you, Frank, but I'll be fine, honestly." He had been so sweet to her. She didn't want to take advantage.

"Nonsense... It's raining," he informed her, pointing to the window.

Maggie smiled. Although she was quite used to walking in bad weather, it was always nice not to have to endure it. "Well, if you're sure?"

He nodded as he ushered her out of the door. He was right about the rain. It was pouring. She climbed into the soft passenger seat, secretly excited that she might get another chance to talk about his latest findings.

The engine purred into action and she breathed in the familiar scent of the luxurious leather and mahogany. Her own car had not been dissimilar all those years ago, before she had gotten with Robert, and she smiled at the memory.

"Lorraine knew all about the deal." Frank grimaced a little as he spoke.

Maggie stared at him.

"Rossington was supposed to be arranging for Jake Parry to buy more land from a local farmer. Seemed he had a written contract all ready for the guy to sign, but it was never completed. There was lots of correspondence between Rossington and Parry, mostly arranging and rearranging meetings with the guy to finalize the details. Trouble was, there was no mention of the guy's name." Frank frowned.

"You think Robert was trying to trick Mr. Parry out of his money?" She narrowed her eyes as she studied him.

He glanced over at her, and she wondered if he was afraid she would be offended by the answer. "It's possible." Frank's voice was clipped.

"Well, Aiden said he was trying to sell land to him without actually owning it, so it's quite probable," she mused.

"That's kind of what we were thinking," Frank admitted. He looked a little relieved that she had been the one to say it. "Lorraine said that after Jake passed away, Rossington claimed that her daddy had promised him some money up front, before the deal was closed. That's why he was sniffing around all the dang time. Lorraine's been stalling him since the funeral, trying to make out it's the lawyer's fault for not releasing all of his estate to her yet. You know, red tape and all that. Truth is, she's searched his records and can't find any mention of a payoff to Rossington. Her legal team's been investigating the case and can't find anything suggesting he's owed a bean."

Maggie frowned as they pulled up outside her apartment block. "It explains why she's so keen to nail Robert, though," she said. "It's one thing for him to fool *her* but to try to fool her *daddy* out of his money is another thing entirely. That girl will want as much ammunition as she can find to fire at him, and I'm only too glad I can provide some."

"Let's get you inside." Frank grinned.

"Really there's…"

Her protestations fell on deaf ears as Frank was already halfway out of the car. She sighed. He really was a gentleman. He even took an umbrella from the pocket of his door and held it for her as she climbed out. She felt a little embarrassed to show him where she lived, and she was surprised that he didn't seem in any hurry to leave, even when she had opened her front door.

"Do you mind if I use your bathroom a second?" he asked gingerly.

She smiled. "Of course not."

It was nice to be home, and she took off her coat as Frank went down the hall. She immediately put the pot on for a hot drink and hugged herself as she remembered that the last time she'd had coffee here, Aiden had made it for her. He hadn't been far from her mind all day, and she was just sorry that he wasn't able to see her again tonight. He had rung her several times, though, and she knew he was thinking of her. Last night had been amazing, and she knew he was as desperate as she was to repeat it soon.

She wandered into her small lounge and put on the lamps as she went over to draw the curtains. The empty Ben and Jerry's container was still on the coffee table, and she smiled when she saw it. The dirty plates had disappeared, and she was glad that the whole place didn't smell of food, as it would have if Aiden hadn't washed them while she'd had her shower this morning. He really was a thoughtful guy.

She straightened up a couple of books on her shelf that had been moved, guessing that Aiden must have been looking through them while she had been getting ready earlier.

"Everything all right?" Frank popped his head around the door.

"Yeah, of course. Do you want a coffee or —?"

"No. I've had my fill for one day. Thanks all the same. I'd best get back. Sylvia will be waiting for me."

She followed him to the door. "Thanks ever so much, Frank."

"My pleasure," he assured her as he left.

She was glad to change out of her clothes and went through to switch on the shower. An ornament had been moved from its position on the window sill and was now sitting on one of the glass shelves that held her bottles of scent and toiletries. She shook her head. Frank must have knocked it down when he'd used the bathroom earlier then replaced it on the wrong shelf. She put it back in its place with a smile. She sure wasn't used to having other people in her apartment.

Chapter Fifteen

Maggie woke early the next morning. She had enjoyed smelling Aiden's cologne on her sheets when she'd climbed into bed, but she really missed him. She was happy to think that soon Rossington would be out of their hair, and they would be able to concentrate on being together as a normal couple. That day couldn't come soon enough.

She made herself some toast and coffee once she was ready, because she still had plenty of time to kill before she left for work. Her gaze fell on her bookcase while she sat enjoying her breakfast, and she thought about Aiden checking out her collection yesterday. He must have been taking another look at her own book, *A Modern Guide to Social Etiquette*, since she remembered it was one of the books that she had straightened up last night. She smiled at the thought. That book had been a fabulous personal triumph for her, and she had planned to continue her writing afterward.

Pulling open a drawer from the coffee table, she found a large notepad that she used to collect her ideas. A flutter of excitement ran through her when she leafed through the pages, and she recalled the joy of writing her first book.

"I'm going to do it again," she told herself aloud. "I'm going to write the next book in the series, and I'm going to get it published, just like the first." A sense of pride filled her, and she sat a little straighter in her chair. She was determined to get back on her feet with or without the money Robert had stolen from her.

She quickly turned to a fresh page and started to write. At first it was just the odd word or idea, but very soon she found herself finishing the page and continuing to the next, and the next.

When she finally looked up, she was horrified to see that she had made herself late. Quickly she put the notepad on the coffee table and went to grab her coat and bag.

It was raining again, so she pulled her hood over her head and shot down the street as fast as she could. She didn't have time to worry about whether she was being followed or spied upon today. All she could think about was that she wouldn't have to do this for much longer – no more early starts unless she really wanted them, no more running through the rain because she couldn't afford a car and no more feeling of dread as she reached the café where she would spend the whole day being unappreciated.

She managed a weak smile as she unlocked the door and let herself in. To be fair, the customers were often quite friendly and the few locals who came in did actually seem to like her. It was just the long hours, little pay and the knowledge that the owner, Mr. Burton, would come in every night and snoop around, checking that she had left everything as it should be and taking the money and cash-register readings from the safe, again ensuring that she had everything in order. She always had the feeling he didn't trust her, although he could never complain that anything was ever out of order.

The morning started with its usual steady trickle of customers who came in for a quick coffee. They hardly ever ordered the complete breakfast, which was a shame, as she enjoyed cooking the eggs, bacon, waffles and all that went into a full English breakfast. The smell of disinfectant soon mingled with coffee and fresh bread as she set about clearing out the kitchen cupboards and giving them a good scrub.

She felt determined that she was going to write her book and get out of that dang job as soon as she could, and the thought spurred her on to give the whole place a good cleaning.

She giggled to herself when she finally stopped for a

break and took a good look around the spotless café and gleaming kitchen. She knew she would have to work there for a while longer yet, but she somehow felt more positive about her future today.

Her good mood only lasted until lunchtime when Aiden's brother, Ben, dropped by to see her. His gloomy face instantly told her that something was wrong, and she felt a thud in the pit of her stomach.

"Coffee, thanks." Ben hoisted himself elegantly onto the stool opposite her at the counter.

She eyed him warily, unsure whether to acknowledge their acquaintance. There weren't many customers left, as the lunchtime trade — such as it was — had all but finished and left by now.

Ben sighed heavily.

"You having a bad day, cowboy?" she asked softly.

He looked up at her with a grimace. "You could say that."

She frowned at him, moving a bit closer to the counter. He was studying her.

"You're Maggie, right?"

She nodded slowly.

Ben looked around the room surreptitiously. "Rossington's planning on marrying Lorraine Parry this Saturday," he murmured.

She felt as though someone had just socked her in the gut. Her mind whirled, and she grabbed for the counter to hold herself up. "B-but that's two days away. How?" Her heart pounded, and she felt herself getting hotter.

Ben scowled. "He's got it all worked out. One of those huge marquee-tent things is being erected as we speak, right on the field we're hoping to buy off of them, just to rub salt into the wound."

Maggie shook her head in disbelief. She knew Ben had taken a shine to the beautiful bombshell, and he would be hurt as hell if she went ahead with the nuptials. Trouble was, she might not have much choice in the matter, knowing Robert. She felt herself tremble with dread. If

Lorraine really was going through with the marriage, she must have a really good reason—or rather, a really *bad* reason, if Robert Rossington was behind it.

"He's got all the legalities in place already. He must have been planning this for a while, just in case his attempt to get the land off of her failed, which it did." He huffed triumphantly, clearly pleased that something hadn't gone Rossington's way.

"But she still doesn't want to marry him." Maggie frowned.

Ben shook his head. "Nope. She's been stringing him along until she could prove what he's been up to. It was the only way she could keep a close eye on him while gathering her evidence. She also needed to make sure he didn't disappear before she outed him. He's been kidding about how he wanted to wed her just so he could get the land off of her. Frank Crowthorne found out the bastard's had some attorney trying to find a loophole in the old man's will that would allow him to get his hands on the land without following through with the wedding."

"I take it they didn't find anything?" Maggie pursed her lips.

Ben shook his head. "Nah. It's a double-edged sword in a way. If he'd found a way, he would have tried to get the land out of her long before now."

"But why the hurry? Why now?" She noticed more of her customers leaving. Now there was just an elderly couple still in at a window table.

"That's what we're all wondering," Ben confided with a shake of his head. "Frank's got his friends trying to ascertain if the guy's in some sort of debt."

"You mean someone might be leaning on him for money?"

Ben shrugged. "It would explain his sudden rush to marry the poor girl."

Maggie sighed.

"There's something else you should know."

Bile rose from her stomach as she stared at him.

"He's invited your parents."

Her mind reeled. "What? Why?" She felt sick. She had no idea Rossington would still be in contact with her folks.

Ben shook his head. "He told Lorraine he wanted to show them how much better he could do for himself." He gulped, looking apologetic. "I–I didn't mean..."

She swallowed hard, trying to stop herself from trembling. "*You* might not mean that, but *he* sure does."

"He suggested that Lorraine ask Josie about getting you to wait on them all. She didn't, of course. We just thought you should know. That's all."

Tears stung the edges of Maggie's eyes, and she was relieved when the last couple got up and left just then. She could just imagine Robert flaunting his new wife in front of her parents—and thinking he could have her wait on them all was just the last straw. A recollection of the horrific scene at the Fieldings' party flashed through her mind as heat rose in her cheeks.

"Look... I'm real sorry. Me and my big mouth... I didn't mean..." Ben was on his feet in a second and he put his arms around her.

"You shouldn't be seen with me," she snapped at him as her whole body tensed.

"Don't worry. Rossington's far too busy shouting orders about wedding arrangements to come around here," Ben replied with scorn.

"Even so. We don't want to ruin our chances of exposing him now, do we?" She sniffed hard, trying to stop the tears from escaping from her eyes. It was no good. As a massive boulder settled in her throat, the floodgates opened and huge, hot drops of despair meandered down her flushed face, like lava from a raging volcano.

Ben hugged her tightly, despite her efforts to shrug him off. She knew that the more kindness he showed her, the more she would weaken and give in to the emotions that were running riot through her whole body. With several hours' work ahead of her, she still couldn't afford to fall apart right now.

"What's Aiden doing?" She wiped her face with her tissue, suddenly wishing it was Ben's brother who was standing so close to her.

"He's gone out with Frank," Ben said. He went back around to the opposite side of the counter, obviously realizing that he wasn't making the situation any easier for her. "Said something about another fact-finding mission." He shrugged.

"I'm really sorry." She noticed how miserable he looked and guessed it must have been hard for him to come out and tell her all this. Aiden had told her how much his brother liked Lorraine Parry, and to have to watch them marry on the land he wanted to own himself would be awful. "There's got to be something we can do."

Ben shook his head. "That's what I'd hoped. I haven't been able to get near Lorraine all day, so I don't even know whether she's got enough evidence together yet. It would be great if we could just expose the bastard before he gets chance to make her walk up that dang aisle." He glanced at her hopefully. "I don't suppose you've…"

Maggie shrugged sadly. "I never got anything concrete against him. I mean, I knew he was lying about the burglary, but I couldn't prove anything with that Taylor guy backing him up."

Ben tutted. "That's what I figured," he admitted.

They both looked up as the door opened, and the local sheriff, Dyson Shearer, sauntered in.

"Wondered if I might find you here," he said, nodding at Ben.

"Is everything okay?" The cowboy frowned as Dyson slid onto the stool next to him while Maggie poured another cup of coffee.

Dyson peered around and seemed glad, though not surprised, to see there were no customers about. "I had a tip-off that there was some kind of row between Rossington and Taylor last night," Dyson told them gravely. "Sounded quite full-on from what the neighbors were saying."

"What neighbors? Was Robert back in Pelican's Heath last night?" Maggie's heart hammered at the thought that he might have been close by while she had been on her own.

"Tell me he wasn't with Lorraine?" Ben's face tightened as he fumed.

Dyson shook his head. "It happened over in Almondine." They both visibly relaxed a little.

"I thought Robert was meeting up with Taylor the night before?" Maggie frowned. It sure looked as though Rossington had been reluctant to give up that necklace.

Dyson pursed his lip. "I guess they could have. They were definitely together last night, though. Witnesses saw them having a good 'ole fistfight on some wasteland behind the bank. Taylor hadn't reported it, though."

"So he's not claiming it was in the line of duty?" Ben scowled.

Dyson shrugged. "Wasn't sure if either of you might know anything. That's all." He took another sip of his coffee.

"I know he's planning on weddin' Lorraine Parry this Saturday," Ben replied, his lips tight with anger.

Dyson didn't look surprised as he nodded. "Seems he's been hoping to get her money out of her without actually marrying the girl, but that ain't gonna happen. It still doesn't explain why he's in such a tearing hurry."

"I don't like it, Dyson. That fuckwad's up to something. I just know it."

"Something's sure lit a fire under his ass," Dyson agreed.

"Do you think maybe he knows Lorraine's not so keen?" Maggie mused.

"Then surely rushing her into a last-minute arrangement is more likely to have her turn tail and run?" Ben sounded annoyed, and it wasn't hard to see why.

"So he's taking one hell of a chance on it." Maggie nodded. "He must be dang desperate to risk losing her altogether."

"Well, if it's just her money he's after, he must be in a real hurry to make some easy cash." Dyson was already getting up, putting his hat back on. "I'll do a bit more snooping, see if I can find out just what the heck he's up to."

"I'd be obliged if you could keep us in the loop, Sheriff," Ben said. "If there's any way I can stop Lorraine from walking up that aisle, I intend to do it, you know?"

Dyson nodded. "I know."

Maggie and Ben stared at each other for a few moments after the deputy had left.

"I'm gonna get back over to the ranch, see if I can keep an eye on Rossington," Ben announced. "I feel happier knowing exactly where he is at all times."

Maggie nodded as they both stood up. She felt better knowing someone had an eye on her ex, too. There was just no telling what the bastard would do next, left to his own devices.

* * * *

The rest of the day dragged by for Maggie. Her mind whirled as she tried to imagine what Robert might be planning—and what hold he might have on Lorraine that would make her marry him, even though she clearly didn't want to. It was very gracious of her to want to expose him for the fraud and cheat that he was, but surely it wasn't worth marrying the scumbag over?

Her heart leapt a little when Aiden called her a while later. She hadn't realized just how much she missed him, but, since the other night, she couldn't get him out of her mind.

"Maggie, are you okay?"

"Yeah, of course." She slid into the kitchen to take the call.

"Ben was worried he'd upset you earlier. He can be a real dumbass at times."

She could hear the concern in his voice. "No, I'm fine. Where are you?"

"I'm at the sheriff's office. What time do you finish work?"

She glanced up at the clock. It had only been a couple

of hours since Dyson had left them. Had he unearthed something already? "About an hour's time."

She heard him muttering something at the other end of the phone, and her stomach churned. "Aiden, is everything all right?"

"Try not to worry, darlin'. I'll pick you up in a while." His voice didn't sound happy, and she noticed her hand tremble as she clicked off the cell.

Luckily there weren't many customers the rest of the day and she felt like she was working on auto-pilot as she wiped down tables and forced herself to smile as she served coffee.

Aiden was true to his word, and she was relieved to see his massive truck pull up in the parking lot as she locked up. He took her in his arms and hugged her closely. She could feel the desperation in his body and hoped they were going to spend the night together. The tight furrows on his brow told her it wasn't the case, though. Something was very wrong.

"We have to get back to your place," he said, planting a quick kiss on the top of her head. "Sheriff's waiting for us with a search warrant."

Chapter Sixteen

"What the hell's going on, Aiden?" she demanded as she climbed onto his passenger seat.

He gunned the engine, wiping a hand through his hair. "Dyson's had a tip-off about something. He just needs to check it out. That's all."

"Something like what? What's he hoping to find?"

Aiden shook his head. "He couldn't say. Cam Taylor's involved, though. He's meeting us there, too."

Maggie felt sick. If that fuckwad had something to do with it, she'd lay a dollar to a penny Robert Rossington was somehow behind it.

"Ben said you were on a fact-finding mission today. Did you find out any facts?" She stared up at him hopefully.

"Yep. Rossington's in a heap of debt," he told her a little warily.

She knew there was something he wasn't telling her. "For Christ's sake, Aiden!" Anger mixed with fear as she waited for him to continue.

"Did you know he had dealings with your parents?" Aiden looked edgy.

Her stomach roiled. "No. What sort of dealings?"

He shook his head. "Some sort of business transactions."

She frowned. "My daddy always said he'd have to be desperate to have anything to do with Robert's business." As the words tumbled out of her mouth, she felt a pang in her heart. She'd had nothing to do with either of her parents since they'd berated her for splitting up with Robert. Her mother had called her a liar because of the things she'd told her about him, and Maggie had been gutted that her own parents would believe Robert over their own daughter. He was a plausible rogue, though. Even *she* had to admit that. If the situation had become so bad that they had turned to Robert for help, then she should have been there for them, no matter what they'd done.

She gasped, putting her hand to her mouth.

"I know you haven't done anything wrong, darlin', so you've got nothing to worry about," Aiden soothed her as they pulled up next to the deputy's SUV right outside her apartment building.

She stared out of the windshield while Dyson talked to a guy she recognized as Cam Taylor. Her eyes quickly darted around looking for Robert, but he wasn't there, thank goodness.

"You ready, sweetheart?" Aiden's voice was calm, though she could tell he wasn't at all happy with the situation.

"Let's get this over with." She couldn't look at him for fear of bursting into tears. She knew he would be supportive and sympathetic, but that wouldn't help her right now. They all followed her as she trundled up the stairs to her front door then unlocked it.

Dyson looked uneasy as he gave her a copy of the search warrant. "We've got reason to believe there's a possibility that an item of stolen property might be hidden somewhere in your apartment," he explained.

Maggie frowned. "What sort of stolen property?" None of it made any sense.

"This." Cam Taylor thrust a rather dog-eared photo of a beautiful pale-blue sapphire necklace at her.

"I've never seen this before," she assured them, stunned.

"I told you," Aiden said rather smugly.

"We need to check it out," Dyson informed them, a little apologetically.

"Whose is it?" Maggie asked curiously. It wasn't unlike the sort of thing she used to wear when she still had money, though she would have preferred pink sapphires to blue.

"Lorraine Parry's. Do you know her?" Cam replied.

Maggie shivered with cold as she stared at him in disbelief.

"Maggie, would you come in here a moment, please?" Dyson had gone on ahead into her bedroom and was calling her through.

A sense of dread filled her stomach, and she just knew what he was about to disclose, though she had no idea how. Her feet felt like lead as she slowly made her way toward him. The deputy was standing in front of her battered chest of drawers, with the second drawer wide open. He was holding a couple of her sweaters in one hand and pointed with the other. In the bottom of the drawer, cushioned on an old tee-shirt, was the necklace.

"Did you find anything?" Cam followed them into the room and gazed into the drawer. He held up the photo. "Yep, that's it all right," he confirmed. "Do you have anything to say, miss?"

She felt everyone's eyes on her as her whole body turned weak and her face flushed. She shook her head dumbly. What could she say? Nothing that would make any difference.

"Maggie, I know you didn't do this—" Aiden began.

"We need to take you down to the office," Dyson interjected as he pulled a plastic bag from his back pocket. He carefully scooped the necklace into it, careful not to touch it with his fingers, and he handed it over to his colleague. "You might need one of these, too. It gets pretty cold in the cells." He offered her the sweaters in his hand with a sympathetic nod.

Maggie could hardly move. Everything seemed to be happening in slow motion around her. Aiden reached over and took the warmest sweater, putting his other arm around her shoulder. She was vaguely aware of him talking to Dyson but didn't take any notice of what was being said. Her brain had turned to mush.

* * * *

She was still in Aiden's arms as the sheriff pulled up outside his office and they all clambered out of his SUV. The cold night air whipped around her, mocking her as she walked, in a daze, up the steps.

Frank Crowthorne was inside the office when they arrived, and she guessed Aiden must have called him.

"Don't you worry, Maggie. We'll soon get to the bottom of this," the older guy assured her when she walked in.

"I'll need a statement from her, Frank," Dyson said as they all took their seats around the deputy's desk.

"Of course." Frank sat at one side of her with Aiden on the other as Cam handed around the coffees from the machine on the side-counter.

"Now, Maggie, I realize this is all a terrible shock for you," Dyson began.

Cam snorted.

Dyson shook his head, rolling his eyes. "Can you tell me anything about this necklace?" He held up the plastic bag.

Maggie cleared her throat, trying to bypass the huge lump that had appeared there. "I've never seen it before," she croaked quietly.

"So you won't be finding her fingerprints on it, Sheriff," Frank added matter-of-factly, then he took a sip of his drink.

Maggie felt a glimmer of hope. Frank was right, of course.

"That don't prove nothin'. She could have worn gloves." Cam looked quite happy with himself as he pointed out the obvious.

Dyson looked a little annoyed but went back to the papers in his hand. "So, I take it you would deny any accusations that you stole it?" he clarified.

"Yes." She nodded.

"Of course you would," Cam derided.

Just then there was a loud commotion at the door, and Maggie gaped when she saw Robert and Lorraine standing there.

"Any news, Sheriff? Oh." Robert didn't even try to hide his delight as he saw them all sitting at the desk, peering at the necklace.

"Oh, no, come on!" Lorraine stared in disbelief.

"Is there something we can do for you, Rossington?" Dyson stood up wearily.

"I'd say there is. We just stopped by to see if you had any news on my fiancée's stolen necklace. It looks like we arrived at just the right time. I trust you've made an arrest?" Robert's eyes bored into Maggie's, and she felt her blood boil. There was no way he wasn't behind all of this. She just had to figure out how.

"Well, I guess this means I can have my jewelry back then? Who found it?" Lorraine asked, looking pointedly at Cam Taylor.

"I did. It was found in Miss Welch's belongings, but we haven't had time to fingerprint it yet, ma'am," Dyson informed her.

"Well, you'd better hurry up then," Robert interjected piously. "We're getting married in just over twenty-four hours. My bride might wish to wear it for the occasion."

Dyson rolled his eyes. "I'll do my best."

"Oh no, it's fine." Lorraine waved a dismissive hand at him. "I shan't be wearing that on Saturday. I'm sure Robert will be buying me something new for the occasion, won't you, dear?" She gave him a smug look, and Maggie relished the way Robert cringed at the suggestion of him parting with his cash.

"I thought you might want it for your something blue? Or something old? Or both?" He always was quick with a comeback, Maggie recalled, though she was a little surprised he would recall the traditional English wedding rhyme she had taught him. She shuddered at the memory. She had been so excited about marrying him at first. It had been all she could talk about. Now all she wanted to do was forget him.

"Well, you've clearly got lots to discuss, so we'll get on here and update you as soon as we've got something definite to tell you," Dyson told them, putting a hand up to stop them.

"Of course. I just need to know who found it so I can arrange the reward," Lorraine retorted.

Maggie watched Robert's chest puff up, and he looked as though he was about to burst.

"What reward?" he demanded.

She had to stop herself from giggling as she watched Lorraine put on an innocent face. "The one I offered for the safe recovery of my necklace, of course," she said nonchalantly. "Who should I make the check payable to?" She stared pointedly at Cam again, and Maggie guessed she was up to something.

"There's no need, ma'am. I found it in the line of duty. As you'll know, law enforcers aren't allowed to accept rewards for doing their job, although it's very kind of you." Dyson smiled at her then frowned as he must have noticed Cam's annoyed expression.

"You offered a *reward*?" Robert was clearly seething as he looked from Lorraine to Cam.

Cameron looked furious but said nothing.

"Of course. You remember, don't you, Deputy Taylor? When I reported it missing, I told you I was happy to offer a handsome reward to whoever found it?" She smiled over at him, seemingly oblivious to the way Cam was staring at her, clearly willing her to stop talking.

"You knew about this?" Robert stared accusingly at Cam, whose face had tensed right on up.

"I don't rightly remember," Cam mumbled.

Lorraine looked shocked. "Of course you do. It was the day Frank came to see you." She nodded over at the older guy, who smirked.

"Yeah, I seem to recall something about that," Frank confirmed.

"I must have forgotten." Cam shrugged.

Dyson yawned as he stretched. "Well, if you folks don't mind, I think I should be getting my prisoner fed and settled for the night. We can continue the interview tomorrow, if you're agreeable?"

Frank nodded. "I think that's a very good idea," he interjected before Maggie could respond.

"Prisoner, eh?" Robert narrowed his eyes at her. "Well, I never thought I'd see the day."

"And we'd best get going, Robert. Lots to do tomorrow, remember?" Lorraine came to her rescue and Maggie sighed gratefully.

"Deputy Taylor, if you don't mind, I'll get this into the safe and get it printed first thing." Dyson picked up the necklace again.

Cam seemed like he wanted to object but obviously thought better of it. He just nodded. "I can stick around for a while, if you like?" he offered.

Dyson looked curiously from his colleague to Robert Rossington and smirked. "No, it's fine. You get on home. I'll call you in the morning with any developments."

Cam seemed disappointed but said nothing. He glanced over at Robert a little warily.

Maggie felt as though she were dreaming as she watched everyone get up and move around her while she stayed sitting at the desk. Robert and Lorraine left, much to everyone's relief, and Frank shook Cam's hand politely. Cam looked surprised, but must have realized it was the older man's way of telling him it was time he left also.

Dyson locked the door after they had all gone and he turned back, grinning.

Aiden took his seat next to Maggie once more. "Are you okay, darlin'?" He put his arm around her, and she snuggled into his comfort.

"Do I have to stay here all night?" Her voice was still croaky.

"I'm afraid so," Dyson replied.

"But I didn't take it," she whispered.

"We know, darlin'," Aiden assured her, holding her a little tighter. "But we have to show Dyson's doing his job to keep everything on the level."

Maggie stared at the sheriff, wide-eyed. "Did you put the necklace in my drawer?"

"No, ma'am," he assured her.

Her mind reeled. "Then who did? Surely you don't think I—?"

"Of course we know you didn't take it," Frank told her. "But we still have to figure out who did. Why don't I go get us carry-out, and we can do a little brain-storming?"

Maggie frowned. "You're staying?"

Frank chuckled. "Just for a while. Sylvia will be waiting for me, so I can't be too late."

"I'll be here, though," Aiden told her gently. "That's all right, isn't it, Dyson?"

"Well now, seeing as you left your car at the apartment, I'm sure everyone will assume that Frank'll be taking you home, so no one's going to know if you're still here after he's left." Dyson grinned.

Maggie felt relieved for the first time in hours. Not only was Aiden staying with her, but they were all going to try to figure out what the hell was going on here.

* * * *

"I know Lorraine's got proof that Rossington took the necklace from her dressing-room, but how could he have got it into the apartment?" Aiden mused as they finished up their meal. "Has he got access to the place?" He turned to face Maggie.

She shook her head. "No. The landlord is the only one with a key, and I'm sure he wouldn't let it out of his sight."

Dyson nodded. "If he did, he'd never get another tenant," he said thoughtfully. "There are strict laws about things like that. Folks like to know that they and their belongings are protected."

"Too right," Frank agreed. "So, Maggie, have you had anyone there who could have put it there? Any workmen? Any guests who might have been able to walk around without you watching them?"

She pursed her lips. "Robert was there the other night, as you know, but I was with him the whole time—and he didn't get anywhere near the bedroom."

"That was the only time he's been there?" Aiden clarified.

She nodded, feeling annoyed that he might not believe her. "I'm not in the habit of asking my ex around, Aiden, despite what you might think."

His hurt expression proved to her just how spiteful she sounded, and she immediately regretted being so nasty.

"I didn't mean—"

"I know. I'm sorry. I guess I'm just a bit edgy is all," she told him, snuggling closer against him. He held her tighter, and she knew he understood, although she didn't like herself for taking it out on him. Aiden had been nothing but supportive, and she had no right to be horrid.

"That was before the necklace was taken, anyhow," Frank pointed out.

"Okay, so what about anyone else?" Dyson asked.

"Only these guys," she told him, shrugging.

"Really?" Aiden looked surprised as he glanced over at Frank.

"Just for a moment," Maggie clarified.

Aiden raised his eyebrows a little more.

Frank sighed. "All right. Yesterday I went in to use Maggie's bathroom after I dropped her home," he admitted sheepishly.

"Her *bathroom*?" Aiden looked incredulous.

"Okay, so maybe there might have been more to it than that," Frank relented.

Maggie stared at him. "What do you mean?"

Frank sighed again. "Maggie, don't get mad at me," he began. "A friend of mine in the attorney's office told me that Rossington was asking around about any possible loopholes in the will Jake Parry left. Seems he was looking for a way of getting his hands on Parry's land without marrying Lorraine. My pal was going to break the news to him yesterday afternoon that the agreement was watertight."

"So that's why he suddenly wanted to marry her so soon!" Maggie felt relieved that at least one mystery had been solved so easily.

Frank nodded. "Looks that way. Anyhow, we were worried that Rossington would be hopping mad when he heard the news, and it occurred to us that he might try to take it out on you or Lorraine."

"That's why you insisted on driving me home last night?" It was all clicking into place.

"Yep. When I got back there, I just wanted to make sure Rossington wasn't going to try anything, like he did the other night, for instance. To be honest, I was actually a little surprised not to find him on your doorstep, but then I wondered if he might have broken in or something. I figured if I went in and used your bathroom, I could just quickly check that everything was okay. I'm sorry." Frank shrugged apologetically.

She smiled at him. "That was real thoughtful, Frank. Thank you." It was good to know she had friends looking out for her.

"I don't know what I was expecting to find—anything from broken furniture and smashed mirrors to the odd item being out of place, I reckon. Anything that would suggest someone had been there." He shook his head.

"I take it you didn't find anything?" Dyson asked.

"Nope. Everything seemed to be in order, not that I knew what the place normally looked like, but there certainly didn't seem anything untoward," Frank replied. "I take it you didn't find anything?" He looked over at Maggie.

She felt a thud in her stomach.

"Maggie?" Aiden frowned at her.

She swallowed hard.

"Did you move an ornament in the bathroom, Frank? A china bird? Not that it matters, I just..." She knew the answer by the look on his face. *Oh no!*

143

"The one on the glass shelf?"

She nodded.

He frowned. "I thought it was odd that it was kept there, bunched up with all your toiletries when there was plenty of room on the other side, but I figured that was how you wanted it." He spoke slowly.

"Anything else, Maggie? Anything at all that was slightly misplaced or missing?" Dyson was scribbling something onto the pad in front of him.

She began to shake her head before the bookcase came to mind. "Just a couple of books, but I thought…" She glanced up at Aiden, who seemed surprised.

"Something was taken from the bookcase?" Dyson clarified.

She quickly shook her head. "No, not missing. A couple of books had been moved slightly. That's all. Like someone had been looking at them and not put them back quite right." She could tell she had been wrong in her supposition that Aiden might have been examining her work, and suddenly she felt stupid for even considering it.

"Was one of them *your* book?" Aiden narrowed his eyes.

She nodded silently.

"It has to be Rossington." Aiden was definite about that. "I don't know how he got in, but it had to be him."

Dyson nodded, making more notes. "So, sometime yesterday after he'd spoken to the attorney, he got into the apartment and planted the necklace before you got home."

"But why move things around? Surely that was just leaving clues? If I'd noticed and called you in, you'd have found it right away." Maggie's mind whirled.

"Sounds like a mind fuck to me," Aiden stated angrily.

Maggie felt bile rise in her throat. Of course! Robert liked to play mind games. She nodded, realizing what a fool she'd been. "I should have known," she moaned. "It's just his style to make me think I'm going mad."

"He's the one who must be mad if he thought that'd work," Aiden assured her.

"It'll be interesting to see if his prints show up on that necklace tomorrow," Frank announced, standing up.

"It won't take long to check," Dyson said as he showed him out.

A call came over the radio just as Dyson returned to his desk. He frowned as he answered it. "Sounds like some trouble over at Almondine," he told them. "I wonder where Rossington's at tonight."

Maggie felt a lurch in her stomach.

"I'll stay here with Maggie," Aiden said.

"Can I trust you not to make a break for it, or should I lock you up?" Dyson grinned.

"We're too close to blow it all now, Sheriff," she assured him.

"Good. I'd better shoot." He threw a key over to Aiden. "Lock up after me. I'll call you when I'm on my way back."

"Sure." Aiden followed him to the door and locked it as soon as he'd left.

"You really think it's Robert and Cam Taylor?" Maggie asked him, wide-eyed, once they were alone.

Aiden grinned. "There's a good chance. Rossington sure didn't look happy about that reward, did he? If he's got an inkling Taylor was planning to cash in on it, he's likely to be after that guy's blood around about now, especially if that fight the other night was about Taylor wanting the necklace for himself. Even a dumbass like Rossington will have worked out why by now." He whipped out his cell. "I'll just have a word with Ben to see if he can check on Lorraine."

Maggie took the chance to freshen up while Aiden called his brother. As she washed her face, she was surprised to see how relaxed she looked, especially given that she was about to spend the night locked up in a police cell. It didn't seem so bad with Aiden there, though. In fact, she relished the opportunity to spend some time with him.

She took the pins from her hair and watched it tumble loosely around her shoulders. She let out a small sigh of relief as the tightness eased.

She smiled at her reflection. Although she had no makeup left on, her face looked flushed and bright. It seemed that Aiden Fielding had a favorable effect on her...

Chapter Seventeen

"You didn't make a break for it, then?" Aiden grinned as she joined him back in the office.

"Well, I considered the window, but it just looked too darn cold and dark out there," she joked.

He laughed. "I'm glad to hear it. Look, I even put the heater on for you." He gestured toward the electric fire, and she was immediately drawn to it like a moth to a flame.

She raised an eyebrow suggestively. "You think I'm in danger of catching my death in here?"

"Not if I can help it. Look, I even brought your extra sweater." He pointed to where he had draped it over the back of her chair on top of her jacket.

"Yeah, I noticed." She sniggered.

"Can't take any chances." He threw an arm around her shoulder.

"Seems pretty warm to me," she said with a knowing grin.

"That's because you've still got all these clothes on." He winked at her, and she felt a fire ignite inside her.

"Aiden, have you forgotten where we are?" She feigned shock and giggled.

"Nope. And I haven't forgotten that we've got the keys and the deputy'll ring when he's on his way back—which won't be for a while yet."

She frowned at him curiously.

"Lorraine told Ben that Rossington disappeared a little over an hour ago after they had a huge row about her offering a reward without telling him. No prizes for guessing where he's gone to. Looks like those guys'll be keeping our sheriff busy for quite a while yet." He grinned.

"Is Lorraine all right?"

"Yeah, Ben's over there now. She doesn't expect Rossington back tonight, and, if he does return, he probably won't be sober." Aiden shrugged.

"You've got this all worked out, haven't you?" Maggie smiled, enjoying the fire in his eyes as he told her his news.

"Oh yeah," he murmured, wrapping both arms around her before taking her lips in a lingering kiss that she felt right down to her core.

The inferno inside her was instantly stoked by her passion and she flushed.

"You getting warmer, darlin'?" He must have noticed her face.

"Yup." She nodded.

"Good."

He peeled off her cardigan before slowly unbuttoning her blouse. Her skin tingled beneath the touch of his warm hands. He continued his careful assault on her lips and she gasped when she ran her hands through his silken hair.

"Think I'm getting a little warm in here, too," he hinted, and she giggled before carefully unfastening his shirt.

She kicked off her boots while he pulled at the zipper of her jeans, and she relished the slightly cooler air on her overheated body as she stood before him in just her bra and panties.

He quirked an eyebrow at her questioningly after toeing off his own boots, and her hands trembled when she reached for his tented Levi's. Sliding a hand behind the zipper to ease it open, she felt the warm velvet of his naked cock, which dripped enticingly over her fingers. She blushed at the realization that he had gone commando again today, and she smiled at the thought. Despite the softness of his skin, his member was rock hard, hindering her efforts to pull the zipper over it.

Aiden chuckled from deep within his throat, clearly recognizing her plight, and he slowly rocked back on his heels, clenching his muscles to allow her a little room to maneuver. Maggie grinned when she managed, at last, to free his huge cock. This was certainly a problem she had never had with anyone before—and definitely not with Robert Rossington.

She knelt in front of the handsome cowboy and peeled his Levi's from his damp flesh, yanking them over his feet with aplomb. Looking up at him, she suddenly felt a little shy. He was so gorgeous and he was completely naked as he stood before her. She breathed him in—a heady mixture of sweat, sex and raw sensuality, the likes of which she had never encountered in her life until him.

Licking her lips, she was delighted to notice that her mouth was directly in line with his inviting member, which twitched in front of her face, beckoning her take a taste. Her eyes momentarily flitted to where it pointed— Aiden's handsome face, which was shining down at her encouragingly.

Leaning forward very slightly, she held his hips in her quivering hands and wrapped her wet lips over his helmet, marveling at how perfectly it filled her mouth. She heard a moan emanate from him, and she echoed it with one of her own, feeling the vibration of her lips against his velvety skin. Aiden must have felt it too, as he immediately ran his hands roughly through her hair.

Empowered by his reaction, she hummed one more time before pulling her mouth from the end of his cock. He jerked as though in disappointment, and she quickly licked the salty length of his shaft. He seemed satisfied and continued to run his long fingers through her waves, a little more gently, as she laved his member, sucking at the delicious juices that were escaping its slit.

"Christ, Maggie," he whispered while her tongue licked at his flesh, and she took his balls, one at a time, into her hot mouth.

She felt his whole body stiffen and she quickly cupped her lips around the top of his cock, kneeling higher so she could feed it right down her throat.

"I'm gonna come." Aiden flinched and loosened his grip on her scalp even more, enabling her to pull her face out of the way if she wanted to. She didn't.

He roared his release as his hot seed gushed down the back of her throat, thick and creamy, soothing her from the inside out, coating her in his nectar, his passion. Maggie had never felt so connected to anyone, and she relished the feeling of being so close to Aiden. She wanted to laugh and cry all at the same time. She sensed every nuance of his reactions to her. A gush from her pussy reminded her that their actions also had ramifications on her own body, and she clenched her thighs together tightly when she felt a hot trickle run down her leg.

Eventually she felt his stiff organ become flaccid on her tongue when it shrank back a little, and she slurped the last of his juices, taking his member in her hands and licking off the last few drops.

"That was incredible," he whispered, his eyes still closed when he ran his finger down her cheek.

She turned her head to kiss his hand, and he helped her to her feet as he slowly opened his eyes and smiled down at her. He crashed his lips down over hers, and he held her tightly, his hot, sweaty body pressed close to hers. His cock felt rock hard against the softness of her pussy, and she was sure he could tell just how wet her panties had become.

With one hand he unfastened the back of her bra and she gasped into his mouth at the relief when her flesh flopped free of its confines. Aiden tugged at the fabric, only allowing a tiny gap of air between them as he whipped away the offending item, before her soft skin was pressed hard up against his ripped chest.

"I want you," he whispered, his voice hoarse.

She nodded, unable to speak. It was enough.

With one arm he swept Dyson's notepad and pen from the desk then gently placed her over the polished wood.

Maggie gulped as she leaned right back and was relieved,

although a little embarrassed, when she felt his fingers yank the panties from her clammy skin. She spread her legs then she gasped. She felt the velvet of his cockhead when Aiden lined his member up to her welcoming hole.

"Hang on."

She felt bereft as he quickly moved away from her and she frowned up when she watched him take a step toward his Levi's. Thank goodness he had remembered. He was already opening the foil packet with his teeth when he returned to his position, and swiftly rolled the thin rubber over his cock before throwing her a salacious wink.

Maggie smiled at him, her chest panting hard with anticipation. She nodded to his questioning look, indicating she was ready, and he groaned when he slid his humungous member into her dripping channel. She forced herself not to tense up because she was stretched beyond belief. The pain morphed into exquisite pleasure as Aiden allowed her time to adjust to his size before slipping into a natural rhythm while he pumped harder and harder into her. She was sure she could feel him right up to her womb, and she clung to his biceps, riveted firmly in position, not that she would want to move, even if she could…ever.

He stared down at her, studying her every expression, and she occasionally lifted a hand from one of his arms to stroke his face or his hair. Keeping his weight off her body, he pounded harder and deeper into her until she screamed her delight when a million stars exploded in front of her eyes. He let out a deafening roar, and she felt his cock impossibly expand, his seed erupting. In that moment, she wouldn't have minded if he had forgotten about the condom all together. There was nothing she would like more than to have his baby. The thought invaded her mind, and she realized she wanted to spend the rest of her life with Aiden Fielding.

"I love you," she screamed over the sound of his groan.

He was silenced in an instant when he stared down at her. "Oh my God! I love you too!" Aiden breathed the words as though his life depended on it, and his expression was a mixture of wonder and relief. "I really love you, Maggie." He whispered the words slowly and purposefully, as though willing her to understand, to believe what he was telling her.

His eyes searched her face, and she smiled, astonished and delighted that they both felt the same way. It hadn't occurred to her until that second that she was taking a risk in telling him how she felt. She had just blurted it out in the moment of recognition.

He encased her lips with his once more, and his whole body merged with hers as he held her tight, kissing and licking every inch of her face, her neck and her throat.

Eventually he stood up, flexing his gorgeous muscles when he stretched his body. He must have caught her watching him because a massive grin spread across his face, and he winked suggestively at her.

"I'd better get cleaned up," she murmured, blushing profusely.

Grabbing her clothes on her way through to the bathroom, she scurried off to have a much-needed wash. She heard him chuckle and knew he would find it odd that she was so modest, having just made love, but it was just the way she was.

There was a small shower cubicle in one corner of the washroom, and the water was cool at first, actually making her shiver as the spray bombarded her overheated skin. Luckily, it soon warmed a little and she was relieved to find a bottle of cheap gel which she used to wash her body and hair.

"Need any help in there?" Aiden's deep voice resounded over the gushing water, and she jumped around to see him leaning against the doorjamb. He had obviously had a shower too, as his hair was wet, and he looked refreshed, but he hadn't replaced his shirt.

"I think I can manage. Thank you," she assured him.

He chuckled. "All right. The sheriff's on his way back.

Said he's got some news for us."

Maggie was surprised for a moment before remembering where they were and why. The horror of spending a night in jail had soon dissipated once she realized she wasn't actually going to be locked up and left alone. Aiden couldn't have been kinder or more thoughtful—even without making love to her—and she would never be able to thank him enough.

As soon as he left, she grabbed a towel and quickly got dressed. Aiden had a cup of coffee waiting for her when she returned to the office.

"Great timing. I just heard a car," he said. "Here. You might want this."

He handed her a comb from his back pocket, and she smiled. Her hair was a nightmare at the best of times, but having just washed it, she knew it would be a real mess without a good combing. She felt so much better for having been able to wash it as well as her body, though. She had sure gotten hot tonight.

Dyson didn't look at all surprised to see her sitting at his desk, drinking coffee and combing sections of her wet hair when he walked in. Neither did he bat an eye at the sight of Aiden without his shirt on.

"Nice and warm in here," the sheriff remarked with a grin.

Aiden placed a mug of coffee in front of him before taking the seat next to Maggie. "So, was it Rossington and Taylor?"

Dyson took a long swig of his drink. "Yup. Of course, they're both claiming it was just some harmless horseplay, but the locals sure didn't see it that way."

"So, it was about that dang reward?" Aiden frowned.

"Oh yeah. According to the witnesses, Rossington was accusing Taylor of trying to wheedle the necklace out of him so he could claim the reward from Lorraine."

"He admitted to stealing it, then?" Aiden looked surprised, and Maggie felt her hopes rise.

Dyson shook his head. "Nah, not a chance. I've got witness

statements, though, which'll stand up in court. I was hoping to take them both in for breaching the peace, but they insisted it was all good-humored and they apologized for any disturbance. I could hardly argue with that, especially as I'd have had to bring them back here, and I didn't think that was entirely appropriate with Maggie being here at the same time."

"Shouldn't the marshal take care of them? After all, Taylor is a law enforcement officer." Aiden frowned again.

"He would, but he's away right now. I'm kind of filling in for him," Dyson replied, shrugging.

"How convenient," Aiden muttered.

"I've got an off-the-record meeting with him tomorrow, then he'll be back for Saturday," Dyson replied. "Never misses a Cavern County wedding!"

"You really think it'll go ahead?" Maggie piped up, still wrestling with the tangles in her wayward curls.

"Whether it does or it doesn't, it'll sure be an interesting day," Dyson told her matter-of-factly. He yawned. "Now, if you good folks wouldn't mind getting off to bed, I've got a big day tomorrow."

Aiden looked up in surprise. "Off-the-record meeting?"

"Just a social chat, I expect," Dyson said. "He's asked me to go meet him, anyhow. Don't know what about." He glanced over at Maggie. "So I hope we can get that statement of yours signed and sealed in good time."

"Yes, sir." She smiled.

"Good. Frank'll be over first thing to witness it all," Dyson said.

"I guess we're sleeping in the cells, then?" Aiden asked.

"'Fraid so. There's only one put-you-up bed in this place, and I'm afraid it's got my name written all over it," Dyson said.

Aiden stood up and grabbed Maggie's jacket and sweater, along with his own shirt and coat. "Think it might be best if we share a cell, Maggie, just in case we need to keep each other warm. You know? I heard it gets mighty chilly down on that end."

Dyson sniggered. "Despite what I said earlier, we do have heated cells, but you folks make yourselves comfortable. As long as you don't disturb me tonight, I don't mind what your sleeping arrangements are."

Maggie followed Aiden to the cells. They both climbed onto a single bed — they had no choice in that matter — then snuggled up together. Dyson had been right about the heating. It was real comfortable, apart from being a little cramped, but she preferred that to being on her own tonight. Aiden's body was warm, and he wrapped himself around her like a huge continental quilt. His heart pounded into her ear, soothing her into a peaceful sleep.

Chapter Eighteen

Maggie was amazed that she actually slept in the next morning. Regardless of the rather snug conditions, she woke up comfortable and warm, still in Aiden's embrace.

"Morning, sleepyhead," he teased from beneath her.

At first she squirmed a little, not wishing to admit to being awake, but then she remembered where she was and almost leaped off the bed. Luckily Aiden had a tight grip on her.

"Hey, I didn't mean to frighten you," he told her, looking worried.

"You didn't," she assured him. "It's just that it's late. I should be at work." Her brain whirled with confusion. "I mean...I'm here. What's going to happen?"

"Well, I'm glad to see there is life at this end, after all," Dyson teased them, walking up the short passageway that led to the cells. The door had been left wide open all night, so their only constraint had been the size of the bed, which hadn't actually proved to be a problem at all.

"She's worried about work," Aiden said as he followed her off the bed.

"It's fine. I told your boss you wouldn't be in today. I said you were feeling poorly." Dyson smiled.

"Thanks." She could just imagine what Mr. Burton would say if he knew she had been taken in on suspicion of stealing. The thought made her stomach churn.

"I brought some warm muffins over, and there's fresh coffee in the pot," Dyson went on. "Help yourselves."

Maggie smiled. It was clear that Dyson didn't really believe any of that bullshit about her stealing the necklace.

Hell, he'd already heard that Lorraine had proof Rossington had taken it himself. It was just a case of going through the motions for the time being.

She and Aiden ate their breakfast at one end of the large desk while Dyson made a few calls. Maggie ran her hand gently over the wood, remembering the last time she had been so close to the desk, and she noticed a snigger from Aiden, which suggested he was thinking the same thing.

"I meant what I said, darlin'," he murmured in her ear.

Maggie flushed. He had said that he loved her. And she loved him. It was unbelievable but true. She beamed at him, suddenly imagining waking up beside him every morning and having breakfast together.

"We'll soon have all this sorted out," he promised her, clearly noticing her looking around the room.

She smiled. She trusted him. When Aiden was around, things never seemed quite so bad, somehow. He had certainly made last night much more tolerable.

"Frank's on his way," Dyson told them as Maggie cleared the desk.

"I'll just go freshen up," she said.

Aiden looked as though he was about to follow suit, but then Dyson called him back. She suddenly felt sick at her stomach as she saw Aiden walk over to the sheriff, and they started muttering something she couldn't hear.

Maggie got washed up as she wondered just what they were talking about. Was she being paranoid? They could be discussing anything.

Frank had already arrived when she emerged from the bathroom a short while later.

"Maggie, how are you?" He put his arms out to hug her, and she breathed in his cologne. Frank looked refreshed and clean, and she wished she was a little less disheveled.

"I'm fine," she assured him with a smile.

"Frank's got some news," Dyson announced as they sat around the table with fresh coffees.

Maggie's gut roiled again, and she guessed this was what

the guys had been murmuring about. Aiden grabbed her hand, and her anxiety ratcheted up another few notches.

"I'm afraid it's not good." Frank frowned from his position opposite her. "Maggie, do you still see your folks?"

Maggie suddenly went cold. He must have noticed her expression as he quickly added "Oh it's okay. They're both fine."

She swallowed hard. Having spent the past couple of years resenting her parents for not believing her when Robert had lied about her, the thought of losing one of them had suddenly seared her heart. She shook her head slowly. "I haven't seen either of them since Robert and I split up," she admitted, instantly feeling a wave of guilt wash over her.

Frank pursed his lips. "It seems your dad has been involved in some kind of deal with Rossington."

Her heart sank at the thought and she just stared at the older man.

"Rossington was supposed to have invested some of your folks' savings for them," he went on.

Bile rose in Maggie's throat as she could imagine the rest. "And lost it all," she finished for him.

Frank nodded sadly. "However, your dad had the good sense to get a decent contract drawn up with one of my colleagues over at the attorney's office, who happened to be a pal of his, so he's got a good chance of getting it all back." He looked a little brighter. "I hear he's been down there instructing his legal team to enforce the agreement to make good the loss."

"So it'll be okay?" She was trembling, not daring to believe it.

"They've got a legal right to have their money returned," Frank said with a grimace, "but it might take some time if Rossington hasn't actually got the funds to back it up."

"But he's got no choice, surely?" Aiden frowned.

Frank sighed. "It's not quite as simple as that, son," he replied. "Morally, he will have to refund the money. It just might take a while. That's all."

Maggie gave a little sigh of relief.

"In the meantime, I believe your parents are finding things quite difficult." Frank looked over at Maggie sympathetically.

She closed her eyes momentarily as the horror of it all hit her like a wrecking ball. A thought suddenly struck her, and her eyes popped open again. "That's why Robert stole the necklace. He was going to use the cash to repay them to prevent them from taking him to court." She felt a germ of hope and excitement as she stared across at Dyson, but she was disappointed when he shook his head.

"Or there's Rossington's version," he said gently. "He's claiming that *you* stole the necklace to raise funds for your parents because of the predicament he'd left them in—a sort of act of revenge against him at the same time."

She leaped to her feet. "No!" she shouted across the table. "How could anyone possibly believe that?" Her whole body glowed like hot coals, and she clung to the edge of the desk to support herself as she suddenly felt weak and helpless.

"It's all right, darlin'. No one believes a word of it," Aiden assured her, then he put his arm around her and helped her back into her seat.

Hot, uncontrollable tears streamed down her cheeks, and she grabbed hold of him as he rocked her gently, cooing soothingly in her ear.

Dyson poured her a glass of cool water that Aiden held to her lips, and she sipped it slowly, forcing herself to focus.

She was aware of muttering and a little movement around her, but she closed her eyes, sobbing inconsolably into Aiden's muscular chest. She marveled at how he managed to stay calm as the steady pounding of his heart reverberated through her, eventually slowing the hammering of her own pulse as though they had morphed into one being.

Whether she had drifted off to sleep or fainted, she wasn't sure, but Maggie awoke lying on the cushioned sofa which also doubled as Dyson's bed when the need arose. Aiden was sitting on the floor next to her, gently stroking her hair. He smiled at her and, suddenly, warmth spread through her whole body.

"Dyson got the results back on the necklace. There were only two sets of prints, Lorraine's and Rossington's." His voice was soft and calming.

Maggie smiled as she slowly sat up. "Then I'm in the clear?"

"Just a little more paperwork in the light of Rossington's further allegations, but you'll be home by supper time," Dyson assured her.

She frowned, looking over at the wall clock. It was almost three.

"I just need to check on a couple of things," Aiden said, "but I didn't want to leave until you woke up. Frank's lending me his truck for an hour."

She felt a hitch in her heart when he stood up to go, and she got up with him. "You're going?"

He threw her a dazzling smile. "Not for long. Just a couple of things I need to do then I'll be right back to pick you up."

He leaned down and gave her a lingering kiss on the lips that speared right through to her core. She smiled up at him.

"Don't worry. I'll look after her for you." Dyson rolled his eyes, clearly quite unperturbed by their show of affection.

"I won't be long," Aiden promised before giving her a quick kiss on the top of her head.

* * * *

Aiden really didn't want to leave his blonde beauty in the sheriff's office, but he knew it wouldn't be long before he was back to fetch her. He grinned as he patted his back pocket where he had hidden the key to Maggie's apartment. She wouldn't be needing it for a while and probably wouldn't even notice it was gone from her purse.

He hummed along to an Alan Jackson song as he drove through the leafy country lanes that led to the Fielding Ranch. It was a good job old Frank had good taste in music!

He was relieved to see that everything seemed to be functioning quite well in his absence, and he skipped up the steps to his cabin. It was good to get into some clean clothes, and he had a quick shave before making his way over to the main house. Josie was waiting for him in her large kitchen.

"I made a chocolate cake," she told him with a smile. "I thought it might welcome her home."

"Great idea. Thanks, sis." He bent down and kissed the top of her head. Josie's hair smelled of citrus, a stark contrast to Maggie's floral-scented tresses. He smiled at the thought. "I'm just on my way over there now. Thought I'd air the place and tidy up a little before she gets let out."

"Those sheriffs aren't exactly adept at housekeeping," Josie replied. "It would be really awful for her to get back to find her stuff strewn all over the place."

Aiden chuckled. "They weren't that bad," he assured her. "Though I thought it would be nicer for her to find it all nice and tidy when she got there — sort of flush out a few ghosts or whatever." He shrugged.

"You really are a thoughtful, guy," Josie teased. "Who'd have thought it? My own brother..."

He laughed. "Yeah, all right." He could feel himself blush a little and quickly looked out of the window for a distraction. "Looks like it's gonna rain," he said. His eyes wandered over to a mass of white in the distance. "Is that the tent for the wedding?"

Josie sighed. "Yeah, that's it. They've been working on it all day. It'll be mighty muddy down there if this weather closes in."

"Especially as it'll probably continue all night," Aiden said.

"And I thought rain on your wedding day was supposed to be lucky." Josie shook her head sadly. "Poor Lorraine."

"She's not really planning on going through with it, is she?" Aiden felt slightly sick at the thought.

"Ben's been over there most of the morning trying to persuade her not to," Josie told him. "Sure seems worried she might be holding out on him over something. He's gone on over to the bank at Almondine now, but he wasn't very hopeful about her when he left. Maybe once she knows Maggie's getting out of jail, she might change her mind. Seemed to think they just didn't have enough evidence against Rossington yet, and she knows if she refused to marry him, he's likely to go to ground. Her lawyers are working flat out to gather all the papers they need to prove he tried to swindle her dad, but she wants to make sure Maggie gets her money back, as well."

"What is it about you determined women?" Aiden shook his head incredulously.

"You know what they say about a woman scorned, bro." Josie punched him playfully on the arm, then giggled.

"And talking of which, I promised a certain young lady I'd be there to collect her once the sheriff had finished that dang paperwork. I'd best get a move on." He kissed his sister on the head one more time. "Thanks for this. You go get your feet up now. Don't want Greg blaming me for your swollen ankles." He picked up the cake and hooted as his sister playfully threw a tea towel at him on his way out of the door.

* * * *

Aiden enjoyed singing along to *Good Time* as he pulled up in the parking lot alongside his own pickup that he'd left at Maggie's place last night. He was still singing when he unlocked the door and let himself in. A shudder ran down his back as he remembered the last time he'd been here, and, after placing the cake and his cell on the kitchen counter, he quickly dived into the bedroom to rectify the mess that had been left. He frowned when he saw there was even more to tidy up than he remembered, and he guessed Cam Taylor must have continued to search for more evidence after they'd left.

A loud knock at the door made him jump while he was folding up some of Maggie's clothes, ready to replace in the drawers, and he went through to answer it.

"Aiden, Josie said you'd be here. I can't get hold of Ben." Lorraine looked ashen as she stared up at him.

"Come on in, darlin'. I was just doing a little tidying. That's all. Is something up?"

She nodded, following him into the bedroom. "Robert's onto us," she blurted out breathlessly. "He found all the papers I'd hidden in my safe. There's messages between him and Cam Taylor planning to take Maggie's money and some stuff about my dad's business that I meant to pass on to the lawyers."

Aiden gawped at her. "Your *safe*? How in hell did he—?"

"I don't know. He must have had another key cut or something. I always keep mine hidden along with these. They're the only things he didn't get his hands on." She held up a computer memory stick and a small SD card. "I never keep all my eggs in one basket," she told him.

"Well, hallelujah for that!" Aiden felt a surge of relief, followed swiftly by something sharp being jabbed into his back.

"Didn't take you for a religious man, Fielding." Rossington's drawl could be heard from just behind the door where he must have been hiding until they were both in place. Lorraine was already in the room, standing by the bed, her eyes burning into her fiancé's. "I'll take those." His voice was a menacing snarl as he reached out his other hand to her.

"Or what?" She clearly tried to sound derisive but couldn't keep the tremble from her voice.

"Or he's a dead man." There was a click when Rossington released the safety catch on the gun that was now pointed directly at Aiden's head. "And I don't think his brother will be too happy about that now, do you?"

Aiden's whole body glowed hot, and he watched Lorraine bite her lip. Her fingers quivered as she reached over and placed the software into his hand.

"I knew there had to be more," Rossington told her with a sneer. "I just figured you'd go running to the other brother — the one you're so fucking fond of."

Lorraine pursed her lips while she panted hard, clearly trying to keep her emotions in check. "You've got what you wanted, now let him go!" she demanded.

Aiden felt Rossington's body tense behind him before the bastard let out a loud guffaw.

"You must think I'm a total dumbass!" he leered.

Aiden bit his tongue to stop himself from affirming the answer, and saw Lorraine open her mouth as though to speak, then stop herself at the last minute. She gave Rossington an incredulous look. He seemed a little taken aback at her expression, then snorted before continuing.

"You really think I'd trust you after this? You've been planning to expose all my plans to alleviate you from your dear old dad's estate and a whole lot more besides." He looked treacherous, and Aiden noticed that Lorraine seemed terrified. It made him wonder what other tactics the bastard had used to scare her.

"So you never really wanted to marry me for love?"

Aiden admired her stalling tactics. He just hoped they might be sufficient to buy him enough time to figure a way out of this dang mess. Rossington appeared to be a little thrown by her question, too. *Good.*

Just then Rossington's phone rang. Aiden held his breath, hoping for a chance to catch the fucker off-guard, but, instead, Rossington ignored it and continued his tirade.

"Love? Your sort don't know the meaning of the word. You're all the same — stuck-up little bitches with more money than sense. If I have to marry you to get my hands on your cash, then so be it, but I'd rather not have all the aggravation, to be honest." He spat the words out as though they tasted sour in his mouth.

"So, because you weren't able to get my daddy's money while he was alive, you thought you'd steal it from me instead? Just like you stole Maggie's money?" Lorraine seemed more furious than sad, Aiden noticed.

"That's about the size of it!" Rossington shrugged complacently.

"Well, at least you won't have to worry about marrying me now," Lorraine derided.

Rossington chortled. "Oh, that's exactly where you're wrong," he announced, digging the gun hard into Aiden's temple. "The only way to get that dang money is to marry you, so that's exactly what I intend to do. Tomorrow at nine-thirty a.m., right in front of your precious boyfriend, on the land he wants to pay me a small fortune for. Just think, every time he sees that field, he can remember our wedding. Won't that be nice?" His snively voice was really grating on Aiden's nerves.

Lorraine looked horrified. "You still think you can marry me after all this?"

"Of course, sweetheart. Like I said, it's the only way to get my hands on your daddy's estate. Don't worry. Once you've signed it all over to me, I *might* think about granting you a divorce. After all, I might not want to be associated with your family once everyone knows that your daddy reneged on our bargain—or that your mother attacked me and will probably end up in a mental home."

Lorraine stared at him with fire in her eyes. "That's a pack of damn lies and you know it!"

"Like I told you before, *dear*, it won't stop everyone believing it, especially when Deputy Taylor backs me up." Rossington sneered.

Aiden couldn't believe his ears. So Lorraine was being blackmailed into marrying the bastard! Rossington would actually discredit her family like that—both parents who couldn't defend themselves. That sure explained a lot.

Just then there was a sound from the hallway, and Maggie

stepped into the room.

"He's got a gun!" she yelled frantically over her shoulder.

Aiden breathed a sigh of relief. She must have given up waiting for him to fetch her and now Dyson had brought her over instead.

But it wasn't Dyson Shearer who appeared in the doorway behind the blonde beauty. It was Cam Taylor.

"What the fuck's going on?" Cam had his gun poised but seemed disappointed at the scene before him.

"Slight change of plan," Rossington told him, a little sheepishly. "They came in while I was looking for evidence."

"You fucking imbecile!" Cam shook his head in disbelief.

"It wasn't my fault. I thought she had the only key." Rossington nodded to Maggie, who stood open-mouthed in the middle of the room.

"*He* took it." Cam pointed to Aiden with his gun before lowering it and replacing it in its holster. "I rang you to say I was bringing her over, in case you were still here."

Aiden frowned. What the hell was Cam playing at?

"Well, I've got all the evidence I need...except that!" Rossington barked at Maggie as she was hurriedly trying to tuck her cell into her pocket.

Cam huffed. "We'll be out of here before anyone comes to her rescue," he claimed, shaking his head. "What're you planning to do? Make a run for it?"

Aiden felt his blood boil at the realization that they were both in on this. He had hoped that Cam Taylor was just a slightly crooked cop who bent the rules a bit to make himself a little cash on the side, but he was clearly much more sinister than that.

"I can't. I've got a wedding to attend to in the morning," Rossington sneered. "Now all we have to do is ensure that none of this lot wreck everything. Get that dang cell off of the bitch. For all we know, she could have recorded us."

Maggie took a step away from Taylor. "You're in this with him?" She stared at him, clearly struggling to compute what was going on.

"That's right, bitch. Now you hand over that cell or you can say goodbye to your lover-boy!" Rossington jabbed the gun into Aiden's head harder, making him wince with the pain.

Maggie was still gaping in disbelief as she immediately passed her cell to her ex.

"You take it," he snapped at Taylor, obviously noticing her ploy to distract him.

Taylor went over and took the cell from her, switching it off as he did so.

"Fucking bitch! I told you she was recording everything. She thinks she's so smart." Rossington's whole body felt rigid against Aiden's, making him glad that the fucker couldn't get any closer to his girl. A glow of pride washed over the cowboy at the knowledge that Maggie had at least tried to gain more evidence.

"You'll have to take him." Aiden could practically see the cogs whirring in Rossington's brain as he snapped out his orders to Taylor. "We've got a wedding first thing." He leered over at Lorraine, who looked like she had been about to object but then clearly thought better of it.

"What about her?" Taylor nodded toward Maggie. "You want me to take her, as well?"

Rossington narrowed his eyes. "Nah. She can watch us get married. Show her what she's missed." Venom dripped from Rossington's lips as he jeered at Maggie.

"And what makes you think she won't rat on us? I know Shearer's out of town, but he and the marshal should be back tomorrow."

Rossington dug the gun into Aiden's head even deeper. "If either of them blab, this one gets it. Simple."

"I still think I should—"

"No! If *she's* not there, questions will be asked. No one's going to miss *him*." Rossington was adamant.

Aiden felt bile rise in his throat. He wasn't sure whether Maggie would be safer with him or not, but he sure didn't like the idea of her facing all this alone. He watched her wringing her quivering hands, her face pale and drawn. Such a change from the gorgeous, relaxed girl who had slept so peacefully in his arms this morning when it had looked as though it was all going to work out. His heart went out to her. Hadn't that bastard put her through enough?

Chapter Nineteen

Maggie stared helplessly as Cam Taylor reached over and grabbed Aiden roughly by the arm.

"You're with me," Cam snarled. "We're gonna take a little ride."

Her heart pounded painfully against her ribs but Aiden threw her a wink, trying to reassure her that it was going to be all right. But it wasn't. How could it be?

"We've got a wedding to plan." Rossington sneered at his fiancée when the front door slammed.

Maggie stared at him in disbelief as she heard Lorraine sigh. He sure seemed determined.

Rossington slung an arm around Lorraine's shoulder. "Now, I sure hope you ladies understood what I was saying back there. One word about this to the cops or anyone else and you can say goodbye to that dipshit. Taylor's got an itchy finger. One word from me and that sorry son of a bitch won't hesitate to pull that trigger. You got it?" His voice was like gravel when he growled at them, and both women nodded silently. "Good. Tomorrow we all act like it's a wonderful occasion, nothing's untoward and we just get on with it. Right?"

They nodded again. Maggie threw a sympathetic smile to Lorraine, thankful that she seemed as committed to keeping Aiden safe as she was. It was one hell of a sacrifice, though, for the poor woman to marry that fuckwad, especially knowing just how cruel he could be. Maggie had known for some time that he had a vicious streak, but she'd never imagined he would have someone murdered or blackmail his way into money. She felt sick when she heard him chortle as he led Lorraine out of her bedroom.

Once they were gone, Maggie ran to the front door and locked it, thankful that Aiden had left the key in the lock. Dyson had explained that he had taken it so he could come in and freshen up the place while she had waited for Aiden to fetch her. In the kitchen, she noticed her boyfriend's cell on the side, a small flashing light indicating that he had a missed call from when she had rung to tell him she was ready. Her eyes fell on the chocolate cake, and she sighed, guessing that it was supposed to be for a celebration. There wasn't much to celebrate now, though, she thought wistfully, while huge tears flooded her face.

She went through to her little sitting room and collapsed on the sofa, bawling loudly as everything rushed through her mind like a giant montage. Her heart ached, knowing that she couldn't call for help, and she had no idea where Aiden had been taken or even if he was all right. She kept reminding herself that as long as she kept her mouth shut, there was a good chance he would be kept alive — for now, anyhow.

* * * *

She must have cried herself to sleep because she woke up in the dark with her throat raw with pain. Shivering, she forced herself to stand up and go into the kitchen where she switched on the light before putting some milk to boil. She felt achy, as well as hungry and thirsty, and she knew it was all adding to her misery.

It was an effort to walk through to her bedroom, but she took a deep breath before striding in and switching on all the lamps. Her stomach roiled when she looked around at the mess, and she guessed that Robert had had a good root through her belongings in his quest for more evidence. She narrowed her eyes, opened the window then quickly bundled her clothes back into the drawers. How had he got in? Her mind whirled as she pulled on some fleece pajamas and wandered back into the kitchen. She poured some cocoa and cut herself a large slice of the chocolate cake. Its creamy texture was soothing on her sore throat, and the warm, milky drink comforted her. Taking her snack into the sitting room, she snagged an old crocheted blanket from the back of a chair and wrapped it around her. The feeling of dread that had been in her stomach since she had awoken was slowly dissipating because her mind whirled with ideas and questions.

Robert said he had all the evidence now, so it looked as though Lorraine must have handed over everything she had. It was just a pity he had noticed her trying to hide her cell. She had switched it to record as soon as she'd heard his voice from the hallway, just as a precaution. When Robert had threatened Aiden, she'd had no choice but to hand it over, though. She had thought that Cam Taylor was going to save the day, however, being a law enforcer and all. She shook her head when she brushed the chocolatey crumbs from her fingers. Taylor had sure disappointed her.

While she had been waiting for Aiden to fetch her from the sheriff's office, Taylor had shown up to speak to Dyson. When the deputy had explained that he had to go out to a meeting, Taylor had offered to take her home so they could lock up the office. Maggie had been sure Dyson wouldn't have let her go with him if he had thought Taylor couldn't be trusted. Although they all knew Taylor wasn't exactly the type to do things by the book, it was widely assumed — as far as she understood — that he was just interested in making a little cash on the side, nothing that would physically harm anyone.

Her thoughts trailed back to the last time Robert had been in her apartment. He had taken the key then, and she remembered being thankful that he hadn't stolen it at the time. She frowned. He *had* had trouble retrieving it from his pocket, though. Of course, he must have used some putty or Play-Doh or something to take an imprint of it so he could get a replica made then let himself back in. That would be how he managed to plant that dang necklace, too.

She took the last of her cocoa to bed with her. It was getting really late, and she had a long day ahead of her — one which would require her to keep her wits about her at all times.

* * * *

With the window still open, Maggie awoke to the birds chirping a few hours later. Her first thought was of Aiden, and she wondered how he would be feeling right now. Yesterday morning, she had woken up in his arms, having made sweet love with him over the deputy's desk. The thought made her smile a little. Everything seemed so much more positive when Aiden was about, somehow. She knew he would be willing her to keep her chin up today and to manage without him. Trouble was that she didn't *want* to have to manage without him — ever! Aiden Fielding was the most adorable, handsome man she had ever met, and she could never forget them declaring their love for each other.

She jumped out of bed, hurriedly closing the window as she shivered against the cold. The world out there looked so peaceful when the sun slowly rose above the houses. Closing her eyes momentarily, she wished her mind was as calm and tranquil as the scene before her, and she knew Aiden would be willing her to keep strong.

While she showered, her mind whirled. Questions would be asked about Aiden's absence. His brother and sister would be worried sick. Hopefully they would have assumed he had just spent the night with her — she wished — so he might not be missed for a while yet. Mr. Burton would think she was still sick, so she wouldn't be expected at the café, although she doubted she would have a job left after all this. She had never taken a day off in her life, and she knew her boss would be livid. Once word got out that she was being questioned about a possible theft, the old cuss would have the ideal excuse to fire her. Somehow the thought didn't worry her half as much as she thought it might.

She put on a pretty dress and cardigan with some flat sandals before tackling her hair. Luckily her locks didn't misbehave as much as usual, and she fastened her hair at the sides with a couple of sparkly clips, letting the rest hang loose. After applying the minimum of makeup, she went through for her breakfast and couldn't resist stroking her hand across Aiden's cell that was still on the kitchen counter.

* * * *

It wasn't long before her cab was arriving at the Fielding Ranch. A funny feeling flooded her stomach as she drove past Aiden's cabin, knowing that he wasn't there. She had already given herself a stiff talking to this morning and she was determined not to let anyone know how distraught she was feeling.

"Hey, Josie. I thought you might need a hand?" She smiled as the pregnant lady came to greet her at the door.

"You're a lifesaver, honey," Josie told her. "My dang body decided that today was a good day to start all this morning sickness malarkey!" She rolled her eyes. "I sure hope the baby doesn't have my impeccable sense of timing."

Maggie giggled. "Well, you just point me in the right direction and go get your feet up."

"I think it's my breakfast that's more likely to come up." Josie chuckled, showing Maggie through to the large kitchen.

She looked around with a smile. This reminded her of the huge house she had grown up in, with its enormous kitchen that always smelled of fresh baking. Trays of canapés were lined up along the counters.

"They've got caterers in for the main meal," Josie explained, "and I heard Robert spent a small fortune having a fancy cake made. I'm just supplying canapés to go with arrival drinks. Trouble is, the smell of those anchovies—" She suddenly darted toward the door, and Maggie snickered as she took off her cardigan and replaced it with an apron.

It had been a while since Maggie had taken the opportunity to garnish tiny morsels of food. The folks at the café would laugh if they could see her now. When she and Robert had first got together, they had entertained all the time, and she smiled as she realized how much she missed all the preparation and planning she used to do.

"I am so sorry," Josie returned, looking pale and weak.

"It's okay. I found some olives and—"

"They look fantastic!" Josie's eyes widened when she saw the trays of perfectly decorated hors d'oeuvres.

Maggie grinned. "Should I take them over?"

Josie's look of appreciation soon turned to one of consternation. She shook her head. "No, no, it's fine, really. Ben or Aiden can take them across. I'm sure that's the last place you'll want to be today."

Maggie was touched by her concern, though she didn't get time to relish it because Josie quickly made a dive for the door again.

Ben arrived a few minutes later with another guy Maggie didn't recognize.

"Hey, darlin'. I didn't expect to see you here today." Ben gave her a knowing wink and looked around the room. "Where's Ade?"

"He went over to Springvale," she said, looking away. "Said he should be back later."

"Dang, I thought he'd be around to help out this morning." Ben rolled his eyes. "Oh, Maggie this is Greg, by the way— Josie's husband."

"Yeah, where is she anyhow?" Greg nodded politely at her before looking around for his wife.

"The bathroom, I think."

Greg tutted. "She's been up and down since three a.m.," he groaned. "Poor thing must be tired out by now."

"I guess that means you are, too," Ben replied. "Why

don't you take some time off, see if the two of you can't get some rest once all this lot's out of the way?" He gestured to the snacks on the counter. "Hey, these look great!"

Maggie felt herself flush a little. "I could help you take them across if Greg needs to stay here?" she offered.

Ben looked surprised. "You sure?"

She nodded.

"That'd be great. I'll help you load up." Greg quickly took a couple of the trays and headed for the door while Maggie followed suit.

* * * *

Luckily, it hadn't rained during the night, and the ground was quite dry and firm. The marquee was enormous and beautifully decorated with red roses that contrasted perfectly with the white tarpaulin.

Guests had already started arriving up by the house and were slowly making their way toward them when Maggie finished laying out the canapés along the trestle tables.

"Damn waiters are late!" She heard Robert's sneer as he entered the huge tent. He looked around and spied her by the hors d'oeuvres. "You!" He pointed to her. "Hand around some of that champagne, will you?" He waved his hand in the vague direction of a salver of champagne flutes before turning back to laugh with the group of men he was with. Considering it was his wedding day, Maggie felt that her ex had made very little effort with his appearance. He usually wore a suit, and this one, though perhaps cut a little more sharply, didn't look much different from his usual workwear. She wondered if it was perhaps because he had never planned to actually go through with marrying Lorraine, after all.

Seething, Maggie took the drinks and offered them around to the guests, conscious of Robert's beady eyes following her around the marquee. She looked around for Ben, but he had disappeared. Probably just as well, she thought. She knew the last thing he wanted was to watch Lorraine marry the wrong man.

It seemed as though Maggie had no choice in the matter, though. She knew that Robert would follow through with his threat if she did anything to upset his perfect day.

After a while, the guests began to flock outside to where the ceremony was to take place. Red-rose-covered arbors outlined the area of freshly mowed grass, and even more roses decorated the back of each chair. An arched pergola stood at the front of the chairs, again swathed in bright red roses.

An orchestra was seated at one side, playing a melody of Beethoven's finest, with a large choir sitting opposite them.

The wine waiters had finally arrived and were busy collecting glasses while the congregation took their places, and Robert slowly shuffled to his position in front of the officiant.

She turned her head when she heard gasps, and she saw Lorraine arrive at the bottom of the makeshift aisle. Maggie felt a pang in her heart as she saw the beautiful woman dressed from head to toe in pure white silk, her expression serene, sad, *resigned.*

Ben was loitering in the background, and Maggie realized that he had probably been with Lorraine, trying to persuade her not to go through with the whole charade. Little would he know that his own brother's life depended on it.

"That could have been you," a soft voice murmured from her side, and Maggie stared at the couple who had taken the seats next to where she stood.

"Mom? Dad?" Her voice wasn't much more than a whisper, and her mouth went dry when she gawped at the parents she hadn't seen for over two years. The last time she had seen them, they had been angry with her, shouting and accusing her of all sorts of things. Now they just looked sad, old, frail.

Everyone carefully stood when a chord was played to signify the start of the ceremony.

Maggie smirked when the orchestra struck up the music, accompanied by the choir with the *Bridal Chorus*. Robert's smug expression told her that he, like most of his guests, no doubt, would be ignorant of the inappropriateness of this particular piece of music. Despite being a well-known wedding march, the music actually originated from the opera, *Lohengrin*, which was a tragic story of loss, infidelity and betrayal. Something told Maggie that Lorraine had chosen it, for all the right reasons!

Lorraine caught her eye when she passed and managed a weak smile. Her face was pale, and Maggie guessed she wouldn't have got much sleep last night.

Robert sneered as Lorraine reached him, and he looked over to Maggie with a supercilious grin. Maggie felt her heart sink even lower. He'd won!

Chapter Twenty

The music stopped and everyone took their seats. Maggie felt a thrumming in her head and grabbed her father's chair for support. Words were being spoken but she couldn't make them out. It was as though everything was happening in slow motion, in a dream—or rather, a nightmare. Just when she thought she was going to pass out, she heard a shout from down the aisle that shocked her to her senses.

"You can't marry him!"

Ben was calling out, while Greg and Josie pleaded with him to stop making a fuss.

"He doesn't love her. He only wants her money!" Ben looked fit to burst into tears as he tore himself out of their reach and ran up the aisle to the bride and groom.

Panic washed over Maggie when she looked over to see Robert's furious gaze boring into her. She shook her head, but she knew there was no way he'd believe that she had nothing to do with the sudden outburst. Hot tears flooded her eyes, and she shook violently as she realized that this could cause Aiden's demise.

"Here. Sit down, love." Strong arms held her, and she smelled her dad's familiar cologne when he helped her into his seat.

She allowed her parents to hold her while she trembled in their embrace, hearing angry, raised voices all around her, none of them making any sense. The officiant was trying to calm everyone down, but the congregation was in uproar. Ben was shouting loudly, pointing at Robert and practically begging Lorraine to think about what she was doing. Lorraine appeared totally horrified while Robert looked like he was about to kill someone. Maggie only hoped that 'someone' wasn't her beloved Aiden.

"I'm sure that's the marshal!"

Maggie heard her dad's surprised acclamation, and she turned to where he was pointing, quickly wiping the tears from her eyes.

Not only was the marshal marching up the aisle, but so were Sheriff Dyson Shearer, and Cam Taylor! Robert seemed enraged at the intrusion. "Arrest that man. He's causing a breach of the peace!" he demanded, pointing to Ben.

The marshal and Taylor had their hands on their hips, not far from their pistols as the sheriff shook his head at the groom. "Robert Rossington, I'm placing you under arrest," he announced, pulling a pair of handcuffs from his back pocket.

"What?" Robert gawped at him, his expression as black as thunder.

"You heard me. And I hope everyone else heard me, too." The sheriff raised his voice, looking around at the congregation as he pushed Robert around to face them. "You are charged with theft, burglary, assault, fraud, intention to defraud, blackmail, intention of false imprisonment, death threats — need I go on?"

"You've got no proof of anything!" Robert blustered.

"No, but I have." Cam Taylor pulled a handful of papers from his pocket.

"You double-crossing..." Robert's words faded into insignificance as another strong pair of arms wrapped around Maggie's shoulders, pulling her gently to her feet.

"Aiden?" She still felt dazed, and now she was sure she was dreaming.

"Yeah, it's me." His dazzling grin lit up his whole face — and her whole world.

"But how...?" It made no sense. Nothing did right then.

"Cam Taylor's a cop, remember? He was stringing that cuss along just long enough to get all the evidence they needed to convict him for a dang long time."

She frowned. "Then he—"

"I'll explain it all later," he promised with a wink. "Right now, I think it's time you introduced me to your folks, don't you?" He nodded to the couple sitting with her and Maggie felt her heart lift.

* * * *

The congregation moved back into the marquee where they all enjoyed more champagne.

Aiden insisted that Maggie have brandy, which he told her was good for shock, while her parents stuck to soft drinks.

"I can't believe we were so taken in by that man," her mom kept saying.

"We all were, sweetheart." Dad put an arm around his teary wife, kissing the top of her head. Maggie smiled. She found it so comforting when Aiden did that to her.

"But we believed him over our own daughter." Mom was really holding back those tears now, and Maggie leaned over to put an arm around her other side.

"It's okay, Mom, really. He managed to trick a lot of people. Look how he fooled me!"

"I'm so sorry," her mom said, hugging her tight. Maggie felt her dad's arms holding her too, as they all squeezed the living daylights out of each other.

Aiden gave them a little space for a while before returning with fresh drinks. Her mom looked a little embarrassed for him to see her puffy eyes and tear-stained cheeks, and she quickly wiped a handkerchief over her face. He must have sensed her discomfort as Aiden took the opportunity to whisk Maggie over to a quiet corner where they stole a few moments for a lingering kiss. It was so good to be back in his arms again, back where she belonged. She never wanted to be anywhere else.

"I was so scared," she confessed, when he finally freed her

mouth. She could hardly believe that he was here—alive! "I really thought he might—"

"I know, darlin'. There was no way of letting you know I was safe. Taylor had to play his part in taking me out of there. He tried to take you, too, but you saw how Rossington reacted to that idea."

Maggie remembered that Cam Taylor had, in fact, suggested taking her, but Robert wouldn't hear of it. She had no idea it was the deputy's way of protecting her.

"I even left my cell at your place, and we couldn't be sure Taylor's wasn't being tracked so I couldn't call you." Aiden grimaced. "He hid me someplace out of town where Rossington wouldn't find me. Then he explained that he wanted to get all the evidence in place so they could arrest him this morning before he tried to ruin Lorraine's life, too."

"So it was all planned out?" She gawped at him.

"He's kind of been working undercover for years," Aiden explained. "Dyson Shearer didn't even know. That's what the marshal wanted to tell him yesterday when they met up. He knew Dyson was as straight as a die and would soon figure that something was off. He just didn't want him to blow the guy's cover before they got everything in place."

Maggie felt her heart hammering as her brain tried to compute everything he was telling her.

"So, when he fabricated my burglary, was that part of the act, too?"

Aiden grimaced. "I'm afraid so. He knew Rossington was a con man. He was hoping to catch him falsifying an insurance claim over that."

"But the claim was in my name. They said I didn't have a case." She felt herself go hot as she recalled that awful time.

"Rossington called your insurance company and inquired about making the claim himself, as the money was in his safe. They turned him down flat, of course. Once he realized he didn't have a leg to stand on he finally gave up. Taylor was gutted!" Aiden shook his head. "The cops have got copies of messages, recorded conversations—everything they need. Taylor was going to 'out' him right after you two split, but then he noticed the fuckwad spending more and more time with your dad. He smelled a rat right away and started digging a bit deeper. He found out Rossington was also doing some kind of scam across Jake Parry. Seems the bastard's got a way of charming himself into business deals he can't uphold. He's totally believable—and an opportunist. Seems he strikes when he knows a guy's vulnerable. For your dad, it was when you two had just split, and he'd convinced your folks you were mentally unstable. For Jake Parry, it was when he started to become ill. With all that going on it seems Taylor dared not expose him too soon, not knowing just how many more irons he had in the fire. He felt real bad about what you had to go through, but he just wanted to get the bastard for all of it. It was the only way to get him the kind of sentence he deserved."

"And will he get my dad's money back now? And Jake Parry's?"

Aiden nodded. "Every last penny, if Rossington hasn't spent it all."

Maggie sighed with relief. It actually looked as though the whole nightmare was finally over. She also had her parents back, which was just amazing. Looking up into Aiden's gorgeous blue eyes, she felt her heart melt all over again. The love that poured from his face wrapped her in a cocoon of warmth and safety. She touched his cheek with the back of her fingers before combing them through his silky hair. To think she could have lost him yesterday was just intolerable. She wouldn't have put it past Robert, though. She had seen the fury in the man's eyes, and it had shocked her to the core.

"I don't think Robert's a sane man," she whispered. "He had a gun to your head. He was planning to shoot you."

Aiden must have seen the tears that filled her eyes, and he took her hand and kissed it gently. "He was just desperate.

He knew we were on to him and he wanted to scare us off, that's all. Taylor got suspicious when he called him and didn't get an answer so he high-tailed it over there to find out what the fucker was up to. You gave him the perfect excuse. I wasn't in any danger once you two arrived."

It was all too much. Maggie clung onto him and cried hard into his muscular chest. His scent, his warmth, his whole being surrounded her, and, for a few moments, she let him wash over her as she cried it all out. Her throat was still sore from last night, but she didn't care. Her head thrummed with all the confusion and worry, but it didn't matter. The important thing was that he was here with her—safe. She couldn't ask for more than that. He held her tightly while she sobbed her heart out then he offered her his large handkerchief. Even that smelled of him, and she breathed him in like he was her last breath. She wiped her face.

"I must look a right state." She grimaced, recalling how much she took after her mother in the puffy eyes department. Neither of them could cry elegantly. It must have been some kind of genetic thing.

"You look beautiful." He smiled kindly at her before kissing her on the top of her head.

A soothing warmth spread from there right down to her toes, and she closed her eyes at the heady sensation. It seemed as though every part of her body had a direct reaction to every part of his. She opened her eyes again to see him looking down at her, patiently waiting while she composed herself. She beamed up at him and took a deep breath. She could face anything with him by her side.

She looked around the marquee that was full mostly of the townsfolk. Frank and Sylvia were chatting over in one corner while a lot of her regular customers milled about. It seemed that all her family and friends were here today.

"Where's Lorraine?" Maggie suddenly realized that she hadn't seen the bride since the sheriff had taken the groom away.

"Probably the same place as Ben," Aiden told her with a wink.

Maggie grinned. She didn't know Ben or Lorraine very well, but she was sure they'd make a fine couple.

"There's Josie and Greg." Maggie was relieved to see that Josie had a lot more color in her cheeks than earlier, as the couple spotted them and waved them over across the tent.

"Greg told me you said I was over at Springvale," Aiden murmured in her ear as they made their way through the crowd.

Maggie looked up at him, blushing slightly at the deception.

Aiden grinned. "How about we keep on letting Josie think that?"

She nodded. In her condition, there was no point in worrying his sister unduly.

"Greg said you got back just in time for all the excitement," Josie gushed as she hugged her brother.

Maggie guessed Josie would have hugged him even harder if she had known the truth about his absence. Josie gave Maggie a hug too. "Thanks so much for your help earlier." She looked a little sheepish.

"I was just glad to be of some use," Maggie assured her. It was true. After feeling so helpless yesterday, it was good to feel needed.

"We only stopped by to make sure Ben didn't kill Rossington," Josie confided. "We knew this was going to be hard for him."

"What's hard?" Ben suddenly appeared behind his sister, grinning devilishly.

Lorraine was with him, blushing profusely.

Both looked a little disheveled and lot happier than before. It didn't take a genius to figure out why.

They all exchanged hugs, then Ben handed around drinks from a passing waiter. "Seems a shame for all this to go to waste," he remarked.

"Yeah, a whole wedding here and no one to make the

most of it," Lorraine agreed.

Maggie felt Aiden's arm tighten around her, warming her to the core. Just having him near made her feel ecstatic. She knew she could never love anyone more. He suddenly moved, handing his glass to his brother, just as her parents came to join them.

"They're right," he murmured into her ear. "It seems a pity to see it all go to waste."

Maggie felt her whole body burn as she watched him kneel in front of her. His hair looked almost white as the sun bounced off his short, tousled waves, and he smiled up at her, his face shining with hope.

"We've got all our kin here, darlin'. It won't take a minute to run down and pick up a marriage license. The officiant's all set up to do his bit. What do you think?" Aiden bit his lip a little nervously. "I guess what I'm trying to say here is, you know I love you, darlin'. Will you marry me, Maggie?"

Carla's Cowboys

Excerpt

Chapter One

It had been a rough couple of days when Carla Burchfield eventually decided to treat herself to a decent night's sleep in a proper bed. The Melrose Motel's dim lights beckoned her and she sighed as she found the entrance and dumped her bags on the well-worn carpet of the dusty reception.

"How long're you staying?" The old man behind the desk looked bored and smelled of stale pipe smoke.

Carla looked around at the run-down building. It wasn't at all welcoming, but the prospect of a real bed made it the most inviting place on earth. "I'm not actually sure. Can I just pay for tonight and take it from there?" She pushed the peak of her cap up a little, trying to assure the guy there was nothing shifty or suspicious about her. In fact, the cap was hiding her greasy, uncombed hair as much as it was attempting to disguise her.

The old guy scratched his white hair and nodded. "Sure. Twenty bucks for the room. If you want breakfast there's a café across the street."

Carla nodded and handed over the money. She'd noticed the café on the way here and been disappointed to find it closed. It was almost ten o'clock and the place was deserted. "Is there anywhere to eat now?" she asked hopefully.

The man shook his head. "Nope. We don't get many people passing through here so there's no need."

She could certainly see why!

She followed his directions to her room, disappointed but not really surprised. Her stomach growled, reminding her that she hadn't eaten since noon. She had a couple of candy bars in her bag and a bag of potato chips that would have to tide her over until morning. She pulled the cap from her head as soon as she was alone, causing her long dark curls to fall manically around her shoulders. She was looking forward to a good shower and the chance to wash her hair. She found the room and quickly opened the door.

The first thing that caught her eye was the bed. It was a single, and the eiderdown looked quite thread-worn and faded, but it made her heart sing. She dumped her bags, locked the door and leaped onto the bed. It was hard but not as hard as the ground she had slept on last night, or the park bench from the night before. She had spent her first night away on the train, which was more comfortable but she hadn't dared fall asleep then.

This felt sumptuous and cozy and she immediately closed her eyes. Relief swept through her whole body and she sank into the lumpy mattress.

She must have fallen asleep as she opened her eyes a while later to find the room in total darkness. Even the dim light that had filtered in from the street when she had arrived had been switched off. She quickly fumbled around for the light switch before pulling off her clothes, and had a wash at a basin in one corner of the room. The nearest bathroom was down the hall, she'd remembered, and she threw on a nightshirt as she went to find it, being careful to lock her door as she left.

As soon as she returned to her room, she rummaged in her bag for her journal, which she wrote as she devoured the snack from her bag. Even the potato chips did little to abate the growls from her empty stomach, and she looked forward to getting a good meal in the morning. She had been so busy concentrating on getting away from Sheridan that she hadn't bothered to stop for proper meals. She'd grabbed whatever she'd been able to at whatever station she had found herself at before hopping on another train. She figured she must have traveled far enough by now, and hoped Jerome and his gang wouldn't think to look for her in South Dakota, let alone a little place like this. It was so out of the way and she had walked for hours since leaving the tiny train station several miles away.

She climbed into the bed and relished the feel of the covers against her tired body. The softness of the pillow and the coolness of the cotton sheets surrounded her in a decadence she had not afforded herself since that dreadful night.

Her mind whirled as she recalled the look on Jerome Pearson's face as he'd celebrated his victory with Quinn Mason and Steve and Oliver Hutchings. They'd bragged about the horrified look on Mr. Roberts' face when they'd pulled out their knives, and had forced him to open his safe as well as his cash till. The drug store had netted them almost forty-seven thousand dollars, and they were planning to split it four ways. Trouble was, they'd been so busy drinking to their success that none of them had been still capable of counting the money, let alone guarding it.

Carla had seen a side to her boyfriend she had never imagined, and in that first few seconds her love and adoration turned to hate and loathing. He was nothing but a common thief who enjoyed tormenting old men, threatening their lives if they didn't hand over the money they had worked so hard to make. She had known Mr. Roberts for several years, and had comforted him at his wife's funeral. Betty Roberts had been a good friend to her when she had first arrived in Sheridan, and she had even given her a job for a while.

Once the men had drunk themselves to sleep she had taken the opportunity to grab the money and run. That money was for Mr. Roberts and she just had to figure out a way to get it back to him without landing herself in trouble. She knew Jerome and his buddies would kill her if they caught up with her, but she had to do *something*. Mr. Roberts didn't deserve this and she was determined to help him.

The memories of that night haunted her dreams and her mind reeled with possibilities as she drifted off to sleep again.

When she woke she actually felt much better. It was already after eight-thirty, and she smiled as she looked around the little room. It was very sparse, with just one old rattan chair in the corner and an even older chest of drawers against one wall. The carpet was worn and the paper was peeling from the walls, but to Carla it was luxury. Even the damp, musty smell that hung heavily in the air wasn't enough to darken her mood.

She felt a lot more human once she had showered and dressed in clean clothes, and she grabbed her bags and headed out to the little café for some breakfast. The smell alone was heaven, and when she saw the size of the portion she was given her heart leaped. She devoured the huge breakfast along with two pots of tea and several slices of toast.

"You look like you haven't eaten in a week." The round lady behind the counter grinned.

Carla didn't want to tell her how long it had been since she'd had a decent meal, so she just smiled and tucked in. She was quite a large girl and could probably do with losing a few pounds, she thought, but there was certainly a limit to how long a girl should go without proper food.

The two bags sat on the bench next to her, one containing the few clothes she had thrown together, and the other with the money. She had stuffed the notes into a duffel bag, hoping it would look inconspicuous, and she guarded it with her life. Until last night that had meant not having a proper sleep in case someone tried to take it from under her head, where she used it as a cushion while the strap was tightly wrapped around her wrist. That was why she had slept so soundly last night, she supposed.

"Is there a bank near here?" she asked the woman, who took her plate away.

"About half a mile away it is," she told her with a smile. "We've got a post office down the road but that's it. Folks don't usually hang about here — they just drive right on through."

Carla nodded. She had looked out for local amenities when she had arrived last night, but in the dark it was hard to see much at all. She paid for the meal and set off for the post office where she bought a large postal box and a black marker pen.

"You from Cavern County?" the young girl behind the counter asked her.

"No, I'm just passing through. If I get this ready to send, will it go in the post today?"

The girl nodded. "Post gets picked up this afternoon. If it's anything valuable you're sending you'll need to fill in one of these."

She handed Carla a form. *Damn!* Not only did it require her to declare the contents of the parcel, but also to give her personal details. She bit her lip thoughtfully. "How far is it to the nearest town?"

"About half a mile in that direction there's a small place called Almondine. There's not much there, just a few shops and stuff. The next town after that's about a mile on, that gets you to Pelican's Heath. It's not much bigger but the people are real friendly there."

Carla thanked her and took the box, hoping that one of those places was where the nearest bank would be. She went back to the motel where she had spent the night.

"Please can I stay another few nights?" she asked the old man, who looked surprised to see her again.

"Sure you can. Pay up front, mind. Your room hasn't been serviced yet so you can stay there if that suits?"

"Great." Checking her wallet, she reckoned she could afford five nights. That should give her enough time to get some much-needed rest and the space to clear her head and figure out her next move. She smiled and took the key from him.

Once locked in the little room, which already felt like home to her, she emptied the contents of the duffel bag into the postal box and addressed it to Mr. Roberts at the Sheridan drug store. She toyed with the idea of sending it, giving false personal information on the dang form, but realized that it would leave a paper trail leading back to the post office — and her whereabouts. Damn! Of course, she would be moving on soon anyway, and had signed in the hotel register under a pseudonym but the post office was bound to have had security cameras that could easily identify her, and it wouldn't take long for Jerome or the cops to track her down. She sighed. Maybe she could find another post office and go in disguise, again giving false information? She'd have to get somewhere a long way from here to do that, just to be on the safe side. Biting her lip, she mulled over the idea. She would give it some more thought, and figure out a way to put the plan into action later.

The box was too big to go back into the duffel bag so she pulled her clothes out of her overnight bag and managed to squeeze the box in there. Then she stuffed her clothes into the duffel. She was disappointed not to be able to fit her diary with her clothing, so she slid it into the hold-all with the box, making a mental note to remove it when she had deposited the bag. She might want to write in it later anyhow, so it would be useful to keep it with her.

Okay, back to plan A.

Taking the overnight bag, she headed back out and set off for the bank. She was used to walking so it didn't take her long to find the nearest town. Almondine was quite busy, and had several large shops. The main road through the town was noisy and people were everywhere. She found the bank at the end of a busy street. It was much bigger than she had expected and she wasn't sure whether that was a good or bad thing.

"I'd like to rent a safety deposit box please," she told the elderly lady behind the counter.

"Of course, dear. How big do you need it?"

Carla held up the overnight bag and the lady nodded. She gave her a key and told her how the system worked.

"You'll need to sign in each time you come," the lady explained, "and it's your responsibility to keep this safe."

It was an unusually shaped key, and Carla attached it to the chain around her neck which held her silver initial pendant. She never took the necklace off and it was long enough to tuck into the top of her T-shirts so no one would notice it anyway.

Carla felt relieved as she locked the bag away in the special box and watched the lady secure it in the bank's vault. It had cost her almost all of her remaining money but it was worth it. She had signed the paperwork with a false name and tucked her copy into her back pocket as she left. Empty-handed, she went back out into the sunshine to explore the area a little. She'd have to make some more cash if she was going to keep running — and she wondered if she should have splashed out on a motel room after all, but she really didn't want to sleep rough again.

The sun was high and she was quite warm in her gypsy-top and jeans. She was wearing boots today, having been in sneakers since she'd left Sheridan. She knew she had a few blisters but nothing she couldn't handle.

Wanting to put some distance between her and the bank, she followed a sign which led out toward the west. Half an hour or so later she arrived in the town of Pelican's Heath. The main street was quite busy, though not half as congested as the last town she had been through. This place had several small shops, a doctor's surgery and what seemed to be a couple of office buildings.

"Good morning." A handsome cowboy lifted his hat and smiled as he passed her.

"Good morning." Carla beamed. He seemed a few years older than her, but a good-looking guy all the same.

Several other townsfolk greeted her as she meandered through the narrow streets. *That girl sure was right about them being friendly around here!* It was a very pretty little town, with mountains in the distance, and fields and hills nearby. She spotted a small diner at the end of what appeared to be the main road through town, and her stomach told her it must be lunch time by now.

She could just about afford some coffee and a burger, which she devoured eagerly. After the breakfast she had eaten she didn't think she could ever eat again, but there must have been something about the fresh air and relief of getting rid of that cash that gave her appetite right back to her. *I'll have to decide how to get the money to Mr. Roberts, but at least it's safe for now.*

"Mind if I join you?"

She looked up into the greenest eyes she had ever seen. A big smile accompanied them and the body attached was to die for. Carla felt a warm, fuzzy feeling in her stomach as she nodded speechlessly and watched the tanned, muscular god sit opposite her. She could smell his spicy aftershave as she breathed him in like he was her life source.

"Hey, Matt, what can I get you?" the young waitress chirped, smiling at him. She must have noticed him arrive.

"I'll take a hamburger, please, Maisie. Easy on the onions, though—I might want to kiss someone before the day's out." He chuckled, and the waitress rolled her eyes with a smirk.

"You want coffee with that?"

"Need you ask?"

She didn't even bother to write down the order, just giggled and headed back to the counter.

"Hi, I'm Matt Shearer. You new in town?" His smile was contagious and his eyes were mesmerizing.

Carla smiled. "Carla Burchfield." The words were out of her mouth before she had time to think — not that it was easy to think with this gorgeous hunk in front of her, anyway — and she silently cursed herself for not changing her name.

"Nice to meet you, Carla." Matt's strong hand was across the table in an instant and she couldn't resist snuggling hers into it as they shook. She felt a jolt of electricity shoot through her as they touched, and the warm feeling inside her ignited into a burning flame. "Are you staying around here?"

Carla was tongue-tied by his beauty. He had thick, dark hair that hung in soft waves around his collar and the stubble on his chin gave him a roguish air that she found totally irresistible. He wore jeans and a gray shirt that was partially unbuttoned, allowing a few dark chest hairs to peep through. She nodded.

His meal arrived and they slowly let go of each other's hand as he took up his cutlery. The waitress smiled as she collected up Carla's used plate, but she didn't speak.

Carla sipped her coffee as she watched the gorgeous guy tuck into his meal.

"So, Carla. What do you do?"

His question threw her for a second and she gasped. "Whatever I can find," she told him as casually as she could.

"There's a job going over at the general store if you're looking for work?" He grinned as he told her, obviously noticing her watch him eat.

He licked his lips slowly, and she felt that fire inside her grow into a raging inferno. She liked the idea of working here and seeing him around all the time.

"Really?" Carla couldn't believe her luck. "I've worked in a drug store before. Think they'll take me on?"

"It's worth a try. Tell you what — I'll come over there with you if you like, and put in a good word for you." He winked and she felt something stir inside her, a little farther down than her tummy. *Oh shit!*

"You don't know me," she reminded him, finishing her drink. "Thanks for the tip off, though, I might give it a try."

She forced her feet to move and took a deep breath as she walked away from Matt Shearer — and temptation!

More books from
Totally Bound Publishing

*When life is full of lemons, a girl has to be cowgirl strong
to make all her dreams come true.*

Sometimes coming home is the best way to heal a broken heart — especially with two ranch hands involved.

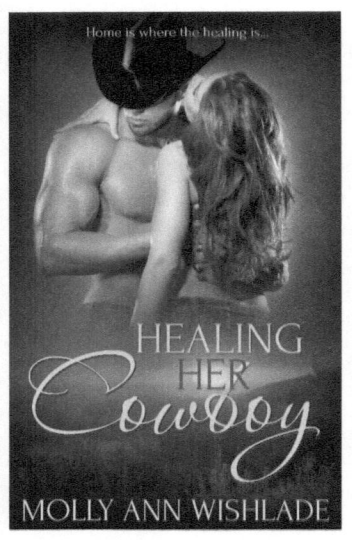

Home is where the healing is.

Three to

FEUD

Now she's back in town, she's all business

NAN COMARGUE

*An old family feud cost Grace the love of two cowboys.
Now that she's back in town, she's all business…but Josh
and Drake are all about pleasure.*

About the Author

Bella Settarra

Bella Settarra is a British Erotic Romance author and lives in the beautiful English countryside.

She has several published novels to date, with subject matter including cowboys, BDSM and Myth/Fantasy. She has also written short stories for anthologies and has even had some raunchy poems published.

She likes to keep busy, cramming as much into each day as she possibly can, while battling — and is determined to win — against breast cancer. She loves to hear from her readers, so please get in touch!

Bella Settarra loves to hear from readers. You can find contact information, website details and an author profile page at https://www.totallybound.com/

TOTALLY
BOUND

Home of Erotic Romance

www.ingramcontent.com/pod-product-compliance
Lightning Source LLC
Chambersburg PA
CBHW020432180626
46812CB00003B/1196